Away in Montana

AWAY
IN
MONTANA

A Paradise Valley Ranch Romance

JANE PORTER

TULE
PUBLISHING

Dedication

To those I have loved
And for those who have loved me
I wouldn't be here without you

Acknowledgements

Thank you to the incredible Tule team for always having my back, and making sure I get the words down and the stories done. I so appreciate the wonderful team, and love working with each of you.

Special thanks to Michelle Morris for reading each chapter and giving me feedback. Invaluable!

Thank you to Lee Hyat and Elisabeth Ringvard for being my first readers and making sure I nailed the ending. Massively grateful!

Thank you Megan Crane for caring so much about everything. You are my wonder girl!

And lastly, thank you to Ty Gurney and my three sons for giving me the time and space to wrestle, pace, panic, and create. This wasn't the easiest story and yet you had such faith in me.

CHAPTER ONE

October 26, 1889

MCKENNA FRASIER SHIVERED as a gust of blustery autumn wind sent red and gold leaves tumbling down Bramble Lane. Her fingers felt cold and stiff from gripping the invitation to Mr. and Mrs. Henry Bramble's Hallowe'en Revels so tightly.

McKenna couldn't remember when she'd last been so anxious about a social event, and that was significant as she'd attended New York costume balls and formal dinners hosted by everyone from the Astors to the Vanderbilts.

She'd once been so fearless.

No, make that naive. She hadn't ever truly understood the rules of New York society, or the consequences, until it was too late.

Dr. Jillian Parker, seated next to McKenna, gave her a light pat of reassurance on her arm. "Don't be nervous. Just be yourself and everything will be fine."

McKenna nodded, and pressed her lips together, wanting to believe Jillian, but as the handsome, red brick mansion at the end of the street came into view, her stomach rose and fell, her thudding pulse now matching the brisk clip-clopping of the horses' hooves.

She couldn't get sick here. It wouldn't do.

Jillian leaned closer to McKenna, her voice dropping so her husband, who was driving the carriage, wouldn't hear. "Mrs. Bramble wouldn't have sent an invitation for the party if she didn't want to include you."

"That's because I forced the issue," McKenna answered lowly.

"You didn't know you were forcing the issue. It was an honest mistake."

McKenna struggled to smile. She knew better.

When the invitation didn't arrive for the Brambles' Hallowe'en party, she shouldn't have asked Jillian to make enquiries. A true lady would have accepted the oversight with grace and quiet dignity, but McKenna being McKenna, didn't quietly accept situations. She had a long history of making mistakes, starting with her childhood. As a girl, she'd been criticized countless times for her strong personality and passionate temperament. Her mother had done her best to teach McKenna that a lady was to always be cool, collected, and self-possessed, and to be fair, she was that... at times. But then there were situations, where she wouldn't, couldn't, accept fate, fighting it, wanting a different outcome.

Like with the Brambles' party.

Heartsick over not being included, she'd approached Jillian Parker—her only friend so far in Crawford County—to discretely enquire about the invitation, wondering if it had gone missing. McKenna was mortified to learn later that the invitation hadn't gotten lost. She hadn't been invited.

She would have cried, if she was a crier.

Instead, she lay awake at night, listening to the wind, the hoot of owls, and the distant howl of wolves, telling herself she was silly to care so much. It was just a party. She'd attended hundreds of parties in the last few years.

During the day, she focused her energy on her pupils, the lessons, and learning how to become a better teacher. It was one thing to study literature and the arts in college, but another to actually teach those subjects, along with math, science, and history.

Just when she'd finally resigned herself to not going, and felt peace about the situation, one of Mr. Bramble's bank employees arrived at the school yesterday afternoon with the coveted invite, and a handwritten note from Mrs. Bramble, asking McKenna to please join them tomorrow, writing that the annual Hallowe'en party wouldn't be complete without her.

McKenna didn't know how to react to the sudden appearance of the invitation. The emotional ups and downs of the past few weeks had rattled her, reminding her of the roller coaster at Coney Island, with all the wild dips and thrills. She'd loved and hated that ride. It had been both exciting and terrifying, and now, looking at the Bramble's imposing, brick mansion in front of her, she felt the same excitement and terror.

They were here.

Jillian flashed McKenna a smile. "Courage," she said.

McKenna managed a matching smile. "Always," she answered breathlessly.

But as they disembarked from the carriage, McKenna's legs felt anything but steady. "What if people know I wasn't supposed to be here?" she whispered to Jillian.

Jillian slid her arm through McKenna's. "There are only three of us that know. You, me, and Mrs. Bramble—"

"And Mr. Bramble."

"Men never know anything about parties. I'm sure Mr. Bramble is clueless." She squeezed McKenna's arm. "So go in, hold your head up, and smile. Give people a chance to get to know you. The *real* you. Not the one people think they know from the newspapers."

"You're so confident."

"It wasn't easy for me when I first moved here. Marietta needed a veterinarian, but they didn't want me. Their new veterinarian was not supposed to be a woman. But I've been here five years now and they've come to accept me. With time, they'll also accept you."

TWENTY-NINE YEAR OLD Sinclair Douglas saw McKenna Frasier the moment she entered the parlor in her persimmon and spice gown, her dark hair pinned up, tendrils already slipping free. Knowing McKenna, those were not artful pieces teased from the chignon, but curls that had already worked themselves loose.

She'd always found it difficult, if not impossible, to contain her intense beauty and energy. Her vivid brightness was both a strength and weakness, and now that she had been exiled from New York, he suspected it'd become an overwhelming liability in Crawford and Park Counties. He'd heard New York society was strict, and punitive, but small towns could be even harsher, and today would be a test. He wasn't sure if she knew there had been a vocal minority who'd protested her hiring, claiming her immorality and scandalous reputation should have made her ineligible for the teaching position in Paradise Valley.

Fortunately, it was just a minority of the community.

Unfortunately, that same minority was present at the Brambles today.

Sinclair had been angered by the barrage of criticism and cruel comments, but there was little he could do without making the situation worse. She wasn't his anymore. And, in hindsight, she probably never had been.

He watched her accept a cup of punch from their hostess. Her hand was not entirely steady as she held the cup. He'd never known her to be afraid of anything before, but then, she'd never been so vulnerable before.

He hated this. Hated that her family had cut her off. Hated that society had cast her out. Hated that she had no one now. But she'd created this situation. She'd made her choice.

His chest squeezed tight and he turned away, retreating into the library where she was no longer in his line of sight.

He wasn't surprised that she still affected him. He'd loved her for so long, it was difficult to not care, but she wasn't his responsibility. She wasn't his, period.

She'd never be his. Not now. And not because he couldn't forgive her—he could do that, and eventually he would—but he didn't trust her. How could a man marry a woman he didn't trust? How could he create a family with a woman who lacked integrity… honor?

He stepped past a cluster of ladies who all paused to smile at him. He nodded, smiling grimly, recognizing all three. One was a married woman, the wife of the reverend, and the other two were young single women who'd taken the train to Montana to find husbands. He knew because the reverend's wife had made several attempts to introduce him to the young ladies.

He didn't like to be rude, but he wasn't interested.

He wasn't sure when he'd be interested in settling down.

He'd been ready a year ago, though. He'd been looking forward to a life with McKenna. They had a future planned out, and he'd purchased land, built a home, saved money for the day he'd need to provide for her.

He'd thought she was looking forward to the same future.

He was wrong.

Sinclair stepped back against the bookshelf to allow a young woman and her mother to pass. The young woman smiled up at him from beneath her lashes. He gave her a brief nod, wishing he was anywhere but here, in an overheated house with too many overdressed people. He rarely attended social events, preferring the solitude of his ranch and his own company, over artificial gaiety and meaningless conversation.

He'd come today because McKenna would be here. He'd come knowing their paths would cross and he thought it was time to put the past behind them, including the accompanying awkwardness. It would be easier once it was behind them.

Or so he'd told himself before he saw her arrive, her dark eyes so expressive, a hint of pink staining her cheeks.

It'd been five years since he'd last seen her and yet he wasn't as detached as he wanted to be.

But it was difficult to be detached about McKenna.

He'd loved her since he was sixteen, almost half his life. It wasn't easy to pretend she didn't matter, and for the past eight weeks, he'd tried to prepare for the moment they would cross paths, having expected it from the time she arrived in Marietta on the train, tensing every time he arrived in town and spotted the swing of an elegant skirt or ribbons stitched against a stylish bonnet.

He'd thought he'd known how he would handle the

meeting—a brief, civil acknowledgment—before continuing on, because he wouldn't cut her. He felt no need to embarrass her or make her uncomfortable, but he certainly wouldn't converse. There was no reason to speak at length on anything. There was nothing between them now. Not even the kisses. Those kisses clearly had meant nothing to her. Those kisses were apparently as insignificant as the promises she'd made him.

I love you. Wait for me. I'll be back soon. There will never be anyone else for me...

And he, naïve boy, had waited. Patiently, because he had to. Patiently, because he wanted to. He'd wanted her to be happy. He hadn't understood her desire to go to college or travel abroad, because people like him didn't do those things. People like Sinclair Douglas filled her father's mines, and worked the smelters, and laid the railroad tracks crossing the West.

But she'd been raised in luxury, spoiled by her doting father, a father who was a self-made man himself, and Sinclair understood ambition, and how Mr. Frasier wanted everything for his daughters, and McKenna, a Frasier to the core, wanted everything, too.

Sinclair had thought he was part of everything, so he'd harnessed his hunger and impatience, encouraging her to study and winter in Italy and summer in England.

While she'd traveled, he'd worked and saved, taking on every challenge, seeking every promotion, knowing if he remained a lowly miner, he'd never get her father's approval to marry her, but if he proved himself, if he rose through the ranks and became a manager, maybe, just maybe Mr. Frasier would respect Sinclair enough he'd consent to the marriage.

Like most miners he knew, he worked seven days a week, and then on the rare day off, he'd write to her, laboring over the letters, rewriting when his sentences leaned too much or he'd dribble ink, smearing the words and staining the page.

Penmanship wasn't his strength. He could read and write, but it wasn't easy for him, not like math. Math was no problem. He'd never met a series of numbers that didn't intrigue him.

But when he sat down to write her, he smashed his insecurity and penned a letter, determined to be entertaining, which wasn't necessarily easy when he worked in the bowels of the earth, but he was good at what he did, a miner like his father. He worked hard, too, just like his father. But he hoped to be luckier than his father who'd died young. Fortunately, his hard work did get noticed, and while McKenna was entering society, he was sent to Marietta to manage Frasier's new copper mine, making him the youngest manager to ever run a Frasier mine.

In Marietta, he wrote her less frequently, not only because her correspondence was more erratic, but he was exhausted. Mining had always been dangerous, but Frasier was pushing the production in the Marietta mine, ignoring safety protocols to meet the nearly impossible quota.

It was better writing to her less often. It meant he didn't have to work so hard to hide his anger towards her father. Frasier didn't seem to care whether his work force lived or died. They were all dispensable, and a new immigrant Finn or Serbian could replace one of his experienced Cornish or Irish workers. It didn't matter if the man left behind a wife and children. It didn't matter if they suffered miners' consumption. It wasn't Frasier's problem. It was Sinclair's. This was why Sinclair had been made the manager, so Frasier didn't have to trouble himself with reality, and practicalities.

So he smashed his frustration, and focused on his job, saving every letter McKenna did write as a testament to the promise she'd made him. She loved him. She'd be back. She was his, and had been his since they were just students in Butte, until gossip reached him in the mines that McKenna Frasier has been disinherited. The Frasier heiress has been disowned.

He didn't believe it. He couldn't believe it. But the scandal filled the papers. People loved to see the high and mighty fall, and no one was higher or mightier than beautiful, wealthy McKenna Frasier.

He hadn't wanted to read the stories. He'd wanted to distance himself from the gossip but, in the end, he'd had to read them. He'd had to understand just how McKenna had become another man's.

And now she was here in Marietta, in the parlor of the Brambles' house, and he realized that as important as she'd been to him, it was time to let her go.

MCKENNA LOST JILLIAN almost immediately after they entered the handsome, red brick mansion, and had been grateful when Mrs. Bramble approached her, warmly welcoming her, and offering her a glass of punch to refresh her after her trip from Paradise Valley.

They visited for a moment, and then Mrs. Bramble was called away and McKenna faced the formal parlor, a faint smile on her face. The Brambles' home was Marietta's grandest, and this afternoon, it appeared that all of the doors of the downstairs rooms had been thrown open to create a series of large rooms perfect for entertaining.

She spied a lavish buffet across the hall in the dining room, while just beyond the parlor, children and adults alike were playing games in the library. The carpet on the opposite side of the parlor had been rolled up for dancing, and a pianist played while a half dozen high-spirited children darted between the adults in a boisterous game of tag.

Bursts of laughter and the hum of conversation drowned out the musicians, but no one seemed to notice. The Brambles' Hallowe'en party, in their grand Bramble House, had become an annual tradition and, from the squeeze, it seemed all of Marietta was here. Outside, crisp red and gold leaves rolled down the lane while inside everything smelled of cinnamon spiced cider and succulent roasted ham.

Encouraged by the laughter and chatter, McKenna approached a group of women, all young mothers with babies in their arms, or toddlers nearby. "Hello," she said with a smile, "I'm McKenna Frasier—"

"I'm sorry." A tall woman in dark blue cut her short. "We're having a *private* conversation."

The other women stopped talking. They all looked at McKenna without expression. For a moment there was just silence, and then one of the babies fussed and the mother shifted the baby to her shoulder, and the women looked the other away.

McKenna's heart did a painful one-two and she dipped her head, holding her smile. "Apologies for intruding." She kept smiling even as she turned away.

Her lips curved as she stared blindly across the room, unable to focus on anything, the rejection so swift it made her head spin and her stomach rise and fall in a nauseating whoosh of sensation.

She shouldn't have come.

She wasn't wanted here.

And, yet, now that she was here, what could she do? Cower in a corner? Run down Bramble in tears? Look for Dr. Parker and beg the veterinarian and her husband to drive her home… a good hour and ten-minute drive?

No, she couldn't do any of those things, and so McKenna kept her chin high, her gaze on the peak of the big mountain rising in the distance. She'd been told once the mountain had just been known as Marietta Mountain, but in the last few years it had been renamed Copper Mountain, after the valuable ore had been discovered.

She focused on the snowcapped peak, her lips tilted, as if enjoying the splendid view in this splendid room.

She smiled as if she was having the most wonderful time, and she'd keep smiling until she returned home tonight, because she'd rather die than let these women know they'd hurt her.

Gracefully, she crossed the room, chin up, head high, until she reached the opposite corner and, once there, sipped her punch and tapped her toe to the music, as if shame didn't threaten to drown her. It was bad enough being shunned by the scions of New York, but to be scorned in Marietta made her doubt her sanity. If she wasn't wanted in frontier Montana, where could she go?

Her emotions rolled, matching her thoughts.

She was beginning to understand. She was finally seeing what she'd missed before.

She hadn't had visitors because she lived so remotely in the valley. Her lack of callers was not due not to the distance, but to *her*.

McKenna's hand shook ever so slightly as she lifted the punch cup to her mouth, pretending to sip, barely wetting her lips as she focused on a group of children bobbing for apples on the far side of the room, needing the distraction to keep tears from welling.

She had not cried since arriving in Montana early August. She would not cry now. And it was foolish to let these people hurt her.

They were strangers. They didn't know her. They didn't know the truth. And she was not about to begin defending herself. Her father might have disowned her, but she was still a Frasier. She knew her value. She had worth. Society—and her father—be damned.

But just thinking of her father put a lump in her throat.

Patrick Frasier had a reputation in New York and Butte for being fierce and driven—overly ambitious—but the criticism was also something of a compliment, as he was a self-made man, a true industrialist and, even more importantly, a doting father. He'd loved his girls, giving them every opportunity, from trips abroad to the best education, including the four years he'd paid for her to attend Vassar College in Poughkeepsie, New York. She'd loved Vassar, and had made lifelong friends there, but her father regretted sending her to college, blaming the liberal education for ruining her.

Education hadn't ruined her. She'd ruined herself trusting the wrong man. Vassar wasn't to blame. She was to blame for thinking all men were men like her father. Or Sinclair.

McKenna swallowed hard again, the lump growing in her throat.

Sinclair Douglas had loved her. He'd wanted her. He'd

waited for her.

But she'd thrown him away, along with every advantage she'd been given. And now she was starting over as a teacher in Paradise Valley's first school, living in the simple log cabin that had been built on the corner of the school property, giving her a place to work and stay. Giving her survival. If not meaning.

At least the worst of the shock was over. She might not yet be comfortable in her new skin, but she'd finally stopped writing her father, begging for his forgiveness, pleading for a chance at reconciliation. She'd stopped writing her younger sister, asking for help. She'd stopped writing her Vassar sisters heartbroken letters. Instead, she sought to amuse them with her adventures on the "frontier". She told them about living in a split log house and cooking over an open fire and trying to wield an ax, and she'd continue turning the struggles into an adventure.

Her friends loved her letters and it felt so much better making them laugh then making them cry. She didn't want or need pity. Her life wasn't over. She refused to be a burden for anyone else.

Mrs. Bramble suddenly appeared at McKenna's side. "Are you not playing games, Miss Frasier?" she asked, gesturing to the game of kissing the Blarney Stone which was now under way in the adjacent library.

McKenna glanced to where the young people were taking turns being blindfolded to try to kiss the white stone in the middle of the library table, and blushing, shook her head. "I'm enjoying watching everyone else," she said.

"Games are a good way to meet people."

McKenna forced a smile. "An excellent point."

Mrs. Bramble smiled back. "The ghost stories will begin soon. Do find a comfortable seat because the curtains will be drawn and the children insist I extinguish all candlelight. They claim they like it spooky. We'll see how they react once it's truly dark."

The hostess moved on and McKenna held her smile, her gaze skimming the room to see if there might be a suitable chair somewhere, when she spotted a tall man in the opposite doorway. He was dressed much as the other gentlemen in a narrow tailored sack suit, with a wingtip collar and a four in hand tie, except he looked nothing like the others filling the parlor and library, and not just because of his height. The breadth of his shoulders set him apart, no padding needed in his jacket to accent his frame. He was muscular through the shoulders and chest, and yet slim through the waist and hip.

She dropped her gaze when she realized he was also looking at her. She'd expected he'd turn away then, but he didn't. She could feel his attention, and she grew warm beneath his intimate scrutiny. He had no manners. Did he think to take advantage of her fallen state?

Finally, she glanced up, straight into his face, thinking she'd give him a measure of her displeasure, but when her eyes met his, her lips parted with shock.

Sinclair.

The room seemed to tilt and shift. Her legs were no longer steady. She put a hand to her middle to try to catch her breath.

She couldn't believe it. She couldn't...

What was he doing here?

She stared at him, astonished. It'd been years since she last saw him, four and a half at least. He'd been a frequent visitor during her mother's illness and then again, after the funeral. But once she'd returned to Vassar, after the end of that awful January, she hadn't seen Sinclair again even though she'd promised him she'd return as soon as she graduated in June.

But she hadn't.

Instead, she wrote him that she'd been invited to travel with friends, and the invitations kept coming. Six months became a year, and then another year, and another.

Heart pounding, McKenna continued to drink him in, noting yet again the fashionable fit of the suit and the crisp white points of his shirt against his skin. He had more color than the last time she saw him. Clearly he wasn't spending all his days underground anymore. His blond hair looked almost brown with the pomade to slick it back.

He was both familiar and unfamiliar at the same time. This afternoon, he wore the suit of a gentleman, but he'd never been a gentleman. He was a miner, one of her father's men. And before her father's man, he'd been her friend.

She sucked in a breath and turned away, looking blindly

for a place to go, somewhere she could hide and recover from the shock.

It was too much, seeing him here. It was too much after everything that had happened.

The scrape of curtains across windows announced the start of the ghost stories. Candles began to be snuffed out.

McKenna slipped from the room, out into the hall, heading for the room upstairs where guests could leave their cloaks and coats. McKenna went there now, not knowing where else to go.

She paced the spacious bedroom twice, a knuckle pressed to her mouth to keep her from making a sound.

Once upon a time Sinclair Douglas had been her world.

Once upon a time, he'd been her sun and her moon and all her dreams wrapped up in one man.

But then she left Montana and discovered the world. And she fell in love with the whole world, realizing it was so much bigger than Butte. Realizing she had so much more that she could want and be, more than just marriage and motherhood. And so she reached for it all, forgetting what happened to Daedalus when he soared too high, flying too close to the sun.

She shouldn't have jumped so high, wanting so much. She should have been content with quiet domestic comforts.

She should have been more like her sister, happy with the hearth, and home.

But she wasn't.

CHAPTER TWO

THE DOOR TO the Bramble's upstairs guest bedroom was open. Sinclair could see McKenna inside. She was pacing, her quick steps carrying her back and forth, heavy skirts swishing, her gown the color of glowing pumpkin with lavish cream lace.

"You look lovely," he said from the doorway.

She stopped short, head lifting, her dark hair curled and pinned high at the back of her head. Rich chocolate wisps delicately framed her face. Her brown eyes met his, and held.

He hadn't meant to say that. He hadn't come to compliment her. And yet it was impossible to deny her beauty. She'd been a pretty girl, and she'd grown into a stunning woman. Some women needed fashionable costumes and elaborate hairstyles to appeal, but McKenna just needed her eyes and smile.

"I'm afraid I'm overdressed," she said, a small catch in her voice. Her fingers flexed before knotting. "I realize now I should have worn something plainer, but it was an autumn afternoon dress, and I thought the spice color would be appropriate." Her husky voice faded and she looked away, her teeth catching at her lower lip.

It was a handsome gown, the color a perfect foil for her gleaming hair. Maybe too perfect. The other women here wouldn't like it. They'd feel plain and insignificant in comparison.

"It would have been," he said bluntly, "in New York, or London."

"So, I have been too conspicuous. I was afraid of that."

"Were you really that concerned?" He walked towards her, a surge of anger rolling through him, making him impatient and harsh. "You've never cared what people thought of you. Why start now?"

She stiffened, pressing her knuckled fists into her skirts. "I've always cared."

"If that was true, you wouldn't be here in your current... situation."

That of a fallen woman.

He didn't say the words, but they hung there, unspoken, in the room between them. Both knew what had happened and what it meant and how it had changed their lives forever.

She surprised him by lifting her chin, a fierce bright light in her eyes. "Alas, I can not change my gown now. What's done is done. Next time I shall wear something with less ornamentation."

She wasn't referencing her gown. She was talking of her fall from grace. He could almost admire her bravado.

Almost.

If she'd been a man, none of this would have mattered. There would have been no fuss. No one would have cared. But she was a woman and her virtue—and innocence—mattered.

Her wealth and her innocence were her greatest gifts. And she'd lost both.

"Perhaps next time you might choose to wear something ready made," he said, "something that isn't couture from the House of Worth?" He saw her surprise and shrugged. "Yes, I'm familiar with Charles Worth and, yes, I know the costume is several years old. But perhaps that works to your favor. No one will think it's an original Worth that way. Instead, they'll think you've copied the design, just as most of America does."

"How is it you've become so knowledgeable of ladies' fashion? Have you left mining to be a tailor?"

"My sister subscribes to *Harper's Bazaar*. She and my mother pour over each issue. I know far more about wool, silk, and horsehair then I ever wanted to learn."

McKenna didn't know how to respond, uncertain if he was jesting.

In Butte, his family had been painfully poor. They were typical of the Irish working class. His father, an immigrant, had died in her father's mine. Sinclair was not yet sixteen when he replaced his father in the same mine, as it was now his responsibility to provide for his family. "How is your mother?" she asked.

"Very well."

"She always was an excellent seamstress."

"My sister is even better."

"Is she?"

He nodded. "Johanna is a dressmaker here, and very good, should you ever need a modiste."

"Johanna is in Marietta?"

"With my mother. I brought them to Crawford County as soon as I could."

McKenna blinked, thoughts racing. "How long have *you* been here?"

"Since early February '85."

"That would have been right after my mother's death."

"Indeed." He paused, studying her, expression inscrutable. "You seem surprised, and yet I wrote and told you." He waited, but she said nothing, and he continued. "I wrote you twice a month for years. Did you even read the letters?"

"Of course I did."

"And yet you didn't know I was in the Marietta copper mine?"

She didn't want to tell him that in his early letters his handwriting had been at times nearly impossible to decipher. The sentences sloped and words inevitably ran together, vowels and consonants so misshapen she'd had to guess at what he was sharing. But she'd taken apart every line and paragraph and then put them back together, creating meaning from context. The latter letters… that was different. "I understood that you'd visited, inspecting the operations. I didn't realize you'd stayed."

"You didn't read my letters."

"I read everything I could."

"Was it such a chore?" he asked, brow lifting sardonically.

"No. Absolutely not. But mail isn't always reliable. There were gaps between letters. Correspondence that didn't come." She didn't add that in the past two years she stopped reading every one, instead opening some, skimming those, before slipping the sheets of paper away. His letters made her feel guilty. She didn't want to be the one to end it, hoping instead he would do it, when he was ready.

"Let me fill you in then. I'll give you the short version. Your father offered me a significant promotion, overseeing the new mine here. I knew then that he thought he was getting rid of me. Imagine his shock when our little mine begins to out perform his in Anaconda. Overnight, I became an invaluable part of his mining enterprise."

She swallowed. "You don't like him."

"He doesn't like me. We are both good with that."

"What has happened?"

"What hasn't happened?" he retorted coldly.

Her pulse jumped and she drew a quick breath, increasingly unease. He was so different. He was harder, sharper, filled with mockery and impatience.

"Did he fire you?"

Sinclair laughed. "No. He'd never do that. I made him too much money."

"You still work for him then?"

"I quit this past summer after an accident killed eleven men and he was more concerned with the loss of equipment then the loss of life." Sinclair paused, broad shoulders shifting. "I wasn't surprised, of course. I knew who your father was, but I'd had enough. I didn't need his money, or his daughter." His voice was hard in the small bedroom. "Even though he dangled both before me, trying to woo me back."

For a split-second she couldn't breathe. Had she heard right? "What is that supposed to mean?" she whispered.

"He offered me a partnership in his company if I'd marry you—"

"Not true."

"Oh, all true. He also put the Marietta mine on the table if I'd save you from your folly." His lips curved. "Such an interesting word for shame, don't you think?"

She stood very still, veins filling with ice.

"All I had to do was take you off his hands," he added. "Did you know?"

She shook her head, feeling faint, too shocked for words.

His lips thinned. "I wasn't flattered by the offer, nor was I impressed with his decision to dump you in Marietta, burying you in a remote corner of the Northwest Territory.

And yet here you are. You managed to find your way to Crawford County on your own."

She took a step back, and then another, until she was pressed against the bed. She leaned against the tall mattress, needing the support. This was so much worse than she'd known. This was… hell.

Sinclair's expression suddenly changed, his brow lowering. "Or did he send you here, to try to win me over?"

McKenna's stomach rose and fell. A lump filled her throat. "*No.*"

"There is no deed for one of the Butte or Great Falls mines in your traveling trunks? No lucrative offer if I marry you and salvage your reputation, protecting the precious Frasier family name?"

McKenna suppressed a shudder as his deep voice scraped her senses. Everything inside of her felt shivery and sensitive, her skin and emotions too bright and alive. From the beginning, he'd brought out the best in her. As well as the worst.

"Why are you doing this? Why are you saying these things?"

"I thought perhaps you were ready to deal with reality. It seems I was wrong."

"You're being needlessly cruel."

"*I* am? What about your father? Is it acceptable for him to dangle you like a treat or a prize—"

"No! It's not acceptable. But he isn't here, and he isn't

the one throwing insults in my face." She pressed her hands to her skirts, trying to hide that she was trembling. "I understand I disappointed you. I understand that he was high-handed and overbearing, but he probably assumed you'd be happy to marry me."

"I'm sure of it. He probably assumed he was doing me a favor. He knew I loved you. I'd approached him years ago, asking for your hand so maybe he assumed I wouldn't care—"

"I didn't know. He never told me." She interrupted before he could continue.

The corner of his mouth lifted. "But I did. In my letters."

McKenna closed her eyes, they burned hot and gritty. She struggled to hold the emotion in, overwhelmed by the shame. "After awhile I didn't read your letters," she said, opening her eyes, looking at him.

He made a rough sound. "I know. It took me a bit, but I eventually figured that one out."

Voices sounded in the hall. McKenna straightened and glanced towards the door. A woman was speaking to a child just outside the door, reprimanding him for being too boisterous indoors.

"I'm sorry," she said softly.

"I know that, too."

She looked at him and he shrugged, his handsome features hard, no softness in him anymore.

"I know you," he said. "You're not a bad person. You

didn't go to New York to hurt me, and you didn't fall in love with... him... to punish me. You just couldn't help yourself."

She went hot then cold. "I kept all your letters." Her voice cracked. She struggled to continue. "I still have them, every single one—"

"Tied up with a delicate red silk ribbon?" He seemed amused now. "My romantic, impractical Miss Frasier. You haven't changed."

"But you have," she said, realizing then he'd known she'd been living in Park County all this time and he hadn't come to see her, nor had his family, even though his sister had once been her friend. "You knew I was here. You've avoided me."

He said nothing and she held her breath, trying to smash the hot, sharp pang in her heart.

He didn't want to know her anymore. They were only speaking now because they were both here, at the Brambles' party at the same time.

It hurt.

She'd never felt more isolated or alone.

He was, she realized, intent on punishing her. Just as a large sector of society wanted to punish her, not because anyone actually knew what she'd done, but over what they suspected she did.

McKenna's hand went to her middle, pressing against the wave of nausea. She couldn't let herself become upset.

She couldn't fall apart in front of him. What did she expect? That he'd be pleased to see her? That he'd wait, like a hound, for her return?

"I should return to the drawing room," she said, blinking to clear the sting from her eyes. "It wouldn't be good for us to be caught alone here."

"And now you worry about your reputation?"

She laughed softly as she turned for the door. "No, sir. I'm trying to protect yours."

THE LOOK SHE'D thrown his way as she walked out was pure McKenna—fierce, defiant, passionate. *Hurt.*

Her gently mocking tone echoed in his head even as he watched the rich saffron silk of her gown disappear around the corner.

It wasn't until he was alone that he exhaled. He'd waited years to see her, and it wasn't the meeting he'd imagined. There was no pleasure in seeing her. Maybe it was because there was no pleasure in hurting her. Even as angry as he was, he didn't like adding to her pain. She was suffering, too. The life she'd known was gone. She had been forced to create a new life, and a new identity, and it wouldn't be easy, not here in Crawford County, Montana.

Sinclair tugged on his tie, and then beneath at his collar, feeling as if he couldn't breathe. But the collar wasn't what was choking him. It was the weight in his chest, the heaviness in his gut.

He was so angry. Bitterly disappointed.

But not just in her. Her father. The world itself.

It would have been better not to see her. He wouldn't feel so conflicted if he hadn't spoken to her. Being near her unleashed emotions he wasn't prepared to feel.

He hated ambivalence. He wasn't built for complicated situations and emotions. He was quite simple, really.

He loved, and he worked, and he worked to take care of those he loved—his family, his country, and his girl. A girl who'd gone away and grown into woman he didn't know.

Today was supposed to have been about closure. He'd come to shut the door on the past, and distance himself from Patrick and McKenna Frasier. He did not work for the Frasiers. He was not beholden to them. He had no need to respect or protect his relationship with any of them. In short, he was a free man.

Of course, it wasn't going to be easy to see her, but he'd known he'd feel better once he'd said his piece, making it clear there was nothing between them. He owed her no loyalty or protection. Whatever they'd had was gone. He didn't care for her, nor did he want a future with her, exhausted by the intensity and chaos McKenna represented.

And then she looked at him, her eyes meeting his, and she dropped the mask, letting him see her—*her, McKenna*—the way he'd always seen her.

Beautiful and brilliant, emotional and passionate, headstrong and impulsive. It made his chest ache. His gut knotted with pain. He could still see the girl in her, and why he'd loved her in the first place.

She was everything he wasn't.

Fiery and funny and so full of hopes and plans. He, who wasn't complex, admired her passion and conviction. He was drawn to her spirit and determination to see the world and change the world and be respected, not because she was a fragile female, but because she was smart and had opinions and believed that she, and all women, were valuable. Not as sisters, and wives, and mothers. But because they were humans.

She was too educated and too headstrong and too rebellious for her own good. The world wasn't ready for her. He wondered if the world would ever be ready for strong, fierce women.

And he'd known all of this when he was eighteen and twenty. He'd known she was so very different from him, but that was what made him want to protect her, and defend her.

And love her.

Sinclair drew a deep, rough breath, wishing he hadn't come today, wishing he hadn't seen that look in her eyes when she realized he'd known she had been here for months, and he hadn't ever tried to see her, or speak to her.

He hated the hurt that darkened her eyes and, yes, it was only there a moment, but it was real, and he felt as if he'd pressed down on a bruise and that made him regret his hard words. She was already struggling. There was no need to rub her face in it.

DOWNSTAIRS THEY WERE telling ghost stories in the darkened parlor and McKenna slipped into a corner. She closed her eyes as she leaned against the wall, the chair rail pressing against her hips, her arms crossed over her chest, the storyteller's words rushing at her, running over her, occupying her brain until her emotions were under control.

But her emotions refused to be controlled. Her heart raced and her pulse drummed and a lump filled her throat, making it hard to breathe.

He'd known she'd been here for months. He'd known she was close and he didn't care.

It hadn't crossed her mind he would even be in Marietta, certain he was in Butte, working one of her father's big mines there.

The lump in her throat grew. Her eyes itched and burned.

She shouldn't have come. She shouldn't be here. She didn't belong here. And everyone at the party knew she didn't belong here, and not just at the Bramble's Hallow'en party, but in Marietta itself. It was such a disturbing discovery, yet another troubling lesson in a year of agonizing putdowns and setbacks.

On the plus side—she wasn't dead yet.

Her lips curved up.

Thank God she still had her sense of humor. It'd saved her before. It might just be the thing that would save her now.

But, seriously, she had to learn from today's humiliation, just as she'd learned from the others. She'd continue to redefine life, sorting through memory and experience, saving the best, relinquishing that which wounded, focusing on who she was now... teacher. Spinster.

She grimaced at that, and opened her eyes to look across the dark, crowded parlor where everyone was quiet and attentive, hanging on the storyteller's next words.

Too bad her students didn't listen to her with the same baited breath. Maybe she needed to read them more Edgar Allen Poe and Mary Shelley.

She smiled as she imagined reading Frankenstein to her students, and just thinking of her students made her think of her school that smelled of raw lumber and chalk and burning firewood. She was lucky to have a job, and she knew it. The work gave her income, allowing her to not just survive, but have a purpose. Teaching gave her meaning, and so she'd continue to focus on her work. She'd read and teach and pour her intense energy into her students.

A light hand touched her arm. McKenna turned her head. Mrs. Zabrinski—the wife of the Russian who owned the local mercantile—gestured for McKenna to follow her. McKenna had met the fur trapper's wife when she'd first arrived in Marietta and needed supplies for her new home.

In the hall, Jenny Zabrinski apologized for stealing McKenna from the entertainment. "Dr. Parker had to leave," she explained, in her lightly accented English. "She was called away on an emergency, and Mr. Parker went with her to make sure she got there safely, but Jillian was quite concerned about rushing away without saying goodbye. She didn't want to leave you stranded. But Mr. Zabrinski and I promised her we'd see you home. There is no reason to worry."

"I'm not worried," McKenna answered calmly, and it was true.

She'd been through far too much in the past year to worry about how she'd get home from a party in town. She was young and healthy and had legs. She could easily walk, and if she left now, she would reach home before dark.

"Nor do you need to trouble yourself getting me home. It's still early and I can easily walk back—"

"No!" Jenny protested sharply, her French accent becoming more pronounced. "You are not dressed to walk such a distance."

"It's just an hour and a half."

"It's at least two hours, and I am sure you're not wearing proper walking shoes. Let me see."

McKenna suppressed a sigh and stepped back so Mrs. Zabrinski couldn't actually lift her hem to check her shoes for appropriateness of footwear. "They're not proper walking shoes, no," she admitted, "but I'm not as delicate as you might think. I grew up in Montana—"

"Yes, yes, you are from Butte, and you are Mr. Frasier's oldest daughter, and he has washed his hands of you." And then she smiled, expression softening. "I know. We all know. But, unlike some, I do not mind. In fact, it makes me like you more. You and I are both the same, outcasts here in Marietta."

McKenna wasn't entirely surprised by Mrs. Zabrinski's admission. She was part Native American, and she'd married a Russian fur trapper. Yes, they'd set up a store in town, and the mercantile was needed, but that didn't make the Zabrinkis part of polite society.

"I don't mind being an outcast if you're one," McKenna answered with a smile. "We can be outcasts together."

"We'll invite Jillian to our meetings."

"Sounds like a wonderful time." She hesitated, remembering why Mrs. Zabrinksi had drawn her from the ghost stories. "Thank you for letting me know Jillian had to leave. I think I'll head out now, too, while it's light—"

"Head out now? While it's still light?" A very deep, familiar voice interrupted her as Sinclair appeared behind them. "You're not thinking of walking on your own, are you?"

McKenna didn't know where he'd come from, or how he'd overheard, but he was the last person she wanted to see or hear from. He'd said quite enough upstairs.

"No," she said flatly.

"*Oui*," Jenny answered, giving McKenna a sharp look.

"I'm fine," McKenna answered fiercely.

Jenny turned to Sinclair. "Mr. Douglas, you live in Emigrant. Can you take Miss Frasier home tonight? She is suddenly in need of a ride."

"What happened to Miss Frasier's ride?" he asked, glancing from Mrs. Zabrinski to McKenna.

"Dr. Parker was called away on an emergency, and I promised the Parkers I would find Miss Frasier a ride home." Mrs. Zabrinski smiled winningly up at him. "I am sure Mr. Zabrinski would be willing to drive Miss Frasier home, but you are going that way, and we live in town, so I thought…" Her voice drifted off but her expression remained hopeful.

McKenna gritted her teeth in frustration. "I do not need a ride, and even if I did, I would not accept a ride from Mr. Douglas."

"Why not?" Jenny asked, surprised.

"Yes," Sinclair added, looking at her now, "why not?"

McKenna could feel the weight of Sinclair's gaze. He was studying her so intently that a silvery shiver raced down her spine, making the fine hair at her nape rise.

But she refused to look at him, focusing instead on Jenny. "I don't want to trouble anyone, and Mr. Douglas no longer works for my father and would probably be quite uncomfortable seeing me home—"

"I'm happy to see you home," he answered, cutting her

short.

Jenny smiled. "See? He is happy to see you home. It is no trouble. In fact, we should do more to take care of you. We are lucky to have you here, teaching the children in the valley. You have a degree, a true college education, from a famous school. The families in the valley are grateful, and I am sure Mr. Douglas is, too, as he will one day have children and his children will benefit from a teacher like you."

McKenna didn't know what to say and couldn't think of an answer. Was Sinclair seeing someone? Was he engaged, or even married? Her stomach lurched, and her heart fell.

"Thank you for the kind words," she said hoarsely, "I'm sure Mr. Douglas doesn't want to leave now."

"Actually, I was just going," he said. "Why don't you say your goodbyes to our hosts, and I'll work on hitching the horse to the buggy."

CHAPTER THREE

H E WALKED OUT the front door, every bit as authoritative and high-handed as her father had been. But he wasn't her father, her husband, or her employer, and she didn't have to answer to him.

McKenna followed Sinclair outside. "Mr. Douglas," she called to him as he passed through the gate to the street. "Thank you for troubling yourself on my behalf, but regretfully, I must refuse your kind offer."

Sinclair stopped walking. He turned to face her, expression blank.

He'd changed so much. He wasn't a boy or a young man anymore. He was a man, a *hard* man, practically a stranger and, for the first time she could remember, he made her uneasy.

She touched her tongue to her upper lip, dampening it, as her mouth had suddenly gone dry. "I shall be taking accommodations in town tonight, and then tomorrow in the daylight, I can walk back or secure transportation home."

He walked back towards her, closing the distance. "There is no place in town that will have you, McKenna."

Her name, spoken in his deep growl of a voice, made her insides twist, ache. His tone was impatient, and rough, and yet he spoke her name as though her knew her.

But he didn't know her, not anymore. Just as she didn't know him.

Perhaps they'd never truly known the other. Perhaps it had all been an illusion. A projection of desire…

"Even if you had the money," he added flatly, coming to a standstill at the base of the stairs, "they wouldn't have you. You are not good for business."

She stood above him, three broad steps between them, and yet he was so tall they were nearly eye level. Her chin rose defensively, her lips pressing tightly. She didn't know this Sinclair Douglas. He wasn't the young man she'd loved. "My father may have disowned me, but the world has not."

"Your father owns the mine, which means he owns more than a fair share of the town. People don't want to alienate him, not when their livelihood depends on him."

"You know that dependence, don't you?" She flashed sarcastically. It wasn't fair of her, but he wasn't being fair, either.

"Too well." His expression hardened. "I resented it at times, but I was also grateful for the work, and the opportunity. I wouldn't have what I do now if he hadn't put me to work." He nodded towards the door. "Fetch your things so we can say our goodbyes."

McKenna was painfully aware of Sinclair at her side as

she buttoned and slipped her soft leather gloves onto her hands. Mrs. Bramble said goodbye at the front door but Mr. Bramble saw them to the gate. "Very happy you could join us," he said. "You will have to come again."

She answered that she would be delighted to pay a future visit, and then Sinclair was ushering her through the gate and to the street where the horse and buckboard buggy waited, the black leather top up, a lantern hanging on a hook.

Due to the tightness of her skirts, McKenna needed his assistance into the practical, black buggy, but she didn't want to take his hand. Being close to him stirred up the past, flooding her with memories and emotions that she wasn't strong enough to manage.

She was quickly learning it was better not to remember the past, or the Sinclair she'd loved. The past was gone and the Sinclair Douglas who'd once made her feel so safe was gone, too.

Her throat worked as she adjusted the ribbon at her chin, retying it more snuggly. She wasn't chilled yet but she would be soon if the wind kept up, and her nerves stretched any tighter. "You know where I live? At the turn off—"

"Yes. I'm five miles southeast of you, in the foothills below Emigrant Peak."

"And your mother and sister? Are they with you, too?"

"No. They're here in town. They live above my sister's shop on Main Street." Sinclair took a seat next to her, and settled a blanket over her legs. "I offered to build them a house on Bramble, but they're not interested, content to be in the thick of things."

He picked up the reins, giving them a brisk flick. The horse responded immediately, and they were off, pulling away from the brick three-story house with the abundance of white trim.

McKenna felt a sudden pang at leaving the luxurious mansion, so like the one she'd grown up in. It was hard leaving a place warm and comfortable, with high ceilings and tall windows that pulled natural light deep into each room. As the day grew later, lights would come on, making the handsome home glow.

The warmth and brightness of Bramble House made returning to her tiny, split log cabin harder, even though she was lucky to have housing provided.

She reminded herself of her blessings now. Work. A home. Relative financial security. At least for the time being.

She was fortunate, too, that she didn't have to travel far each day to teach. But living alone wasn't easy for her. She'd never lived alone before, always having family around her in Butte, and then her friends at Vassar, and then she had her father's extravagant home on Fifth Avenue filled with staff, her father's periodic presence, but lots of friends. McKenna had enjoyed a busy social life and many friends....

She swallowed hard, chin lifting, annoyed by her self-pity. It felt indulgent. She couldn't allow herself to be indulgent, and loneliness wouldn't kill her.

At least, it hadn't killed her yet.

"Comfortable?" Sinclair asked abruptly, his deep voice both a pleasure and a shock every time he spoke to her.

He'd changed so much in the past four years. He'd always been tall, but he'd put on muscle, his frame heavy and powerful, a testament to the physicality of his work and the grueling decade working the Frasier copper mines.

"Yes, thank you," she answered.

Even though they weren't touching, she could feel Sinclair next to her, his energy and warmth tangible, making her heart race and her skin prickle with awareness.

Nervously she smoothed the blanket across her lap. Adrenalin hummed in her veins as leaves swirled down the street, dancing in and out of the horse's hooves.

She'd overheard woman at the party speaking of the weather and what a lovely, long Indian summer it had been with unusually warm temperatures stretching into early October. McKenna had enjoyed the fine weather, too, but in the past couple of weeks, the weather had changed, the cold snap turning the thickets of aspens in Paradise Valley from green to glowing clusters of amber and orange.

"Did you enjoy yourself today?" Sinclair asked, breaking the silence.

She almost laughed at his question. *Did she enjoy herself?*

She pictured the women who'd rebuffed her, entire groups of women who'd turned their backs on her, shutting her out, and then she remembered Jenny and Jillian who'd both confessed they were outsiders, too. It should make her feel better, not being the only one excluded, but having grown up included, it was hard to accept being pushed to the outside. Perhaps if it had been her choice, it'd be different, but she'd made a misstep, and that error in judgment had cost her everything.

McKenna blinked to clear her eyes. Her head suddenly ached. She realized she was tired.

She hated being dependent on others.

She hated being poor.

Hated her disgrace.

Worse, she hated that she'd wanted so desperately to be included today. She'd hoped that the party would help ease her into society. She'd hoped that today women would discover she wasn't scandalous at all, but rather, pleasant company, an educated lady with exceptional deportment.

"It was a mistake to go," she said. "I was not wanted there."

"You were invited."

"I forced Mrs. Bramble's hand." She saw his swift side glance and she gave a half-nod. He knew the worst of her. He wouldn't be shocked. "I wasn't meant to attend. I didn't know that when I asked Dr. Parker to approach Mrs. Bramble on my behalf, but I soon discovered I wasn't meant to be on the guest list."

"Yet you were here today."

She shrugged wearily. "My inquiry put Mrs. Bramble in

an awkward position and so she invited me at the last minute."

"Nobody has to do anything, particularly the Brambles. Your father might own the mines, but Mr. Bramble heads up the bank and they have tremendous influence in town."

"Which is why I couldn't turn the invitation down, once it arrived yesterday. But I deeply regret asking Dr. Parker to speak with Mrs. Bramble. It was bad form on my part."

"You've always broken the rules.

"There are just so many in life and most of them are ridiculous. For example, if women go to medical school they are every bit as qualified as men to—"

"I wouldn't go far."

"You don't even know what I'm going to say!"

"The world isn't ready for women physicians. I'm not ready."

"Women are every bit as intelligent as men."

He shot her a dry look. "I don't doubt that women are intelligent. But women are also emotional and impulsive—see, you're getting upset? You can't get upset every time someone disagrees with you. You'll never win an argument like that." His mouth curved in a faint smile. "How did we even get on this subject?"

"I don't know, but I think you're wrong."

"I'm sure you do," he flashed, before adding, "We were talking about you forcing Mrs. Bramble's hand."

"And I did."

"It's just an afternoon party. No harm done."

"Oh, I'm not so sure about that. The ladies didn't want me there. I tried several times to approach women and was rebuffed." She drew a quick sharp breath. "Half the town made their fortunes in my father's mine, but now I'm beneath them."

"He has distanced himself from you, and so they feel obligated to do the same."

"I've done nothing to them, though."

"Society is punitive, and there will always be those who enjoy another's misfortune. It is human nature."

"I don't like human nature. It's cruel."

"Of course it is. Survival of the fittest. Only the strong survive—"

"I despise Mr. Darwin."

His lips twisted. "Because you've been crushed?"

"I'm not crushed!"

"Good. Remember that."

For several minutes they traveled in silence. She focused on the crunch of leaves and the last glaze of light illuminating the mountain peaks, trying to find comfort in the surrounding beauty. It was beautiful here, too, the mountain peaks far more majestic and dramatic in Crawford and Park County then where she'd lived in Butte.

"It was your doing, McKenna."

Her name, spoken in that low, rough voice, made the air catch in her throat, and a shiver race through her.

"And yes, people judge," he added, giving the reins a flick and propping a boot on the buckboard. "They did in Butte. They did New York. And they will here." He briefly glanced her way. "Imagine if the situation was reversed. Wouldn't you find it satisfying to see someone so exalted fall?"

"I wasn't exalted."

"You were one of the most privileged women in this country. I am sure society here followed your ascent, just as they did in Butte, reading how at first you were snubbed by the old guard in New York, taking Mrs. Astor's lead, calling you 'too ambitious, too wealthy, too vividly beautiful, and too spirited' to know your place, before Mrs. Vanderbilt took you under her wing, ensuring your success."

She shivered a little as he quoted from William Mann's *Town Topic.* "Ava Vanderbilt wasn't accepted in the beginning, either."

"But she had Mr. Vanderbilt's funds." He gave her a cool glance. "Money is power."

She didn't answer. There was no need. Both knew she could have survived the scandal if her father had stood by her. Instead, he'd turned his back, disinheriting her. Money *was* power, and suddenly she had none.

He turned his horse onto the hard flat dirt road that would carry them from town into the rugged mountain valley. If they traveled past the road that led to the school and her cabin, they'd reach Emigrant, and then Cinnabar,

Gardiner, and finally Yellowstone. She'd been born in Montana and she'd traveled extensively abroad, but she'd never been to Yellowstone to see the geyser and hot springs.

"You don't need to take me all the way to the school," she said. "You can let me out on the main road. It's just a short walk from there."

He made a low sound that was almost like a growl. "I'm not leaving you on the side of a road, McKenna."

"I don't like putting you out, or taking more of your time—"

"You're being insulting now."

"I'm serious. There was no need to trouble yourself on my account."

"No? Then how were you to get home tonight, seeing as your *friends* had already left?"

She heard the way he said friends. She knew what he meant. He didn't think much of them for leaving her.

"There was an emergency," she answered, unwilling to criticize Jillian, the only friend she did have.

"They left you stranded." Sinclair's voice was hard, sharp.

McKenna looked away, not wanting to argue.

But her silence only frustrated him. "Did they not care that you'd have no way back?" he persisted. "It's a good distance to your cabin, over an hour at a brisk pace, and even in a wagon, still quite dangerous at night."

"There was an emergency," she reiterated. "Dr. Parker is

a veterinarian—"

"Livestock is important, but you're far more valuable than a barnyard animal."

Heat rushed through her. Her chest grew tight. "I don't know what to say. I'm overwhelmed by the generosity of your compliment."

"If I wanted to pay you compliments, I would. But I'm not trying to flatter you. The road to Cinnabar is difficult at best during the day, and downright treacherous at night. Wolves, bears, along with desperate, amoral men all to happy to prey on vulnerable travelers." His narrowed blue gaze swept over her. "I'd think you'd know that by now. I'd think you be cognizant of the dangers, but what do I know? You've never had to deal with reality—"

"How quickly the compliments turn critical," she interrupted fiercely. "I can't wait to hear what else you have to say to me. Do continue. I am all ears, as well as a captive audience."

"Fine, as I do have questions, and since we have time, you can answer them. So what did happen?" His hard voice sliced through the lavender twilight.

"To us?" she asked unsteadily.

He made a low mocking sound. "There was no us—"

"Not true—"

"If there had been we would have been married by now, with babies and a big place of our own." His gaze swept over her. There was little sympathy in his eyes. "What happened to your lover? Where did he go?"

She blushed and could feel the heat in her face, her cheeks suddenly burning. "He wasn't my lover."

Sinclair gave her another long look. Clearly he didn't believe her.

She gripped her hands together, fingers tightly clenches. "Is this why you offered to see me home? So you could do this? Interrogate me?"

"You don't think I deserve answers? Or, at least the illusion of an apology?"

Her hands balled into fist so tight that it made her knuckles ache. "I'm sorry to have disappointed you."

"When did you know you'd never be mine?"

"*Sinclair.*"

"At Vassar? After?"

"There wasn't a moment," she answered tersely, frustrated. "It wasn't intentional."

He shot her a look of disbelief.

"You know I very much… cared… for you."

When he said nothing she drew a swift, shallow breath. "I did care. Very much." Her voice broke. She gave her head a slight shake, holding the tears at bay. "My feelings were real."

"So what happened?"

"We were apart a great distance, and then separated for too long."

"You could have come home."

She had no answer for this. He was right. It had been her

choice to stay away, enjoying the city, and the pleasures of society.

She'd loved New York. And for a period of time, New York had loved her back. For those two, three years she'd felt as if she held New York in the palm of her hand.

She'd been the dazzling debutante, McKenna Frasier, heiress to the great Frasier copper fortune.

She had friends and suitors and an endless stream of invitations to parties and balls and rides in Central Park.

There had been trips to the Continent, and lavish staterooms on lavish steam ships. Clothes, jewels, box seats to every play, opera, and ballet. She'd had it all.

She could have married anyone—German barons, English dukes, American tycoons. They'd all sought her out, courted her, asked her father for her hand, and she'd refused each, taking her advantages for granted, confusing prestige with protection, and with one misstep her world of privilege was gone.

Swallowing hard, she glanced at him. "I did stay away," she said after a lengthy silence. "And you're right. As time passed, I realized I had no intention of marrying you."

He gave no indication that he'd heard her, but she knew he had.

"I'm sorry, Sinclair," she whispered, balled hands pressed to her thighs, trying to hide the face that she was shaking. "I truly am," she added. "You deserved better."

Finally he spoke. "You're right, McKenna. I did."

CHAPTER FOUR

FOR LONG MINUTES there was just silence. The uncomfortable silence made the trip excruciating. Sinclair ground his jaw tight, wishing he hadn't said anything, aware that McKenna was sitting exquisitely still next to him, her hands clamped in her lap, as if a marble statue.

McKenna was never still. She was energy and motion and her quiet ate at him.

Hell.

Stirring restlessly, he placed a boot on the buckboard, his mind working, wondering if he should say something conciliatory to ease the tension, or if he the issue was that he hadn't said enough.

He was still angry, and more than that, embarrassed. He felt stupid. He'd been a fool waiting for her all those years.

She'd stopped reading his letters years ago and yet he'd continued to write them. And even when he'd begun to have doubts, he hadn't given up on her. He didn't know how to give her up. She'd been a light and a compass. She'd given his life meaning. She'd kept him going.

But he shouldn't have confused inspiration with reality.

He should have realized years earlier that Patrick Frasier's privileged daughter was never going to marry him. He was nothing but a diversion.

In school, he'd been mocked by a principal for being a dumb ox. Brawn, but no brain. Ironically, it was what made him so good in the mines. He possessed remarkable strength, and was able to work hard without asking too many questions.

He should have asked McKenna the hard questions and not waited like a faithful hound at the door.

Thank God the only ones he'd confided in had been his mother and sister. Thank God not even his family knew about his folly—that he'd actually approached Patrick Frasier and asked for his daughter's hand. It was bad enough having Frasier laugh in his face. It would have been worse if others had known.

Frasier's laughter had followed Sinclair out of the room, but that hadn't dissuaded Sinclair. He continued to wait for McKenna.

He cringed, remembering.

Finally, thankfully, they approached the lane for the school.

He directed the horse to turn, the bridle and harness clanking as they traveled east through a thicket of aspens and evergreens to a clearing, moonlight illuminating a clapboard school house and further off to the side, a simple cabin.

Drawing to a stop, Sinclair heard the rushing water of

the Yellowstone River. He knotted the reins and assisted McKenna down, an owl hooting overhead.

Sinclair's gaze swept over the cabin's sturdy split logs and steeply pitched roof. The building was dark, no light glimmering from behind the wooden shutters covering the two narrow windows that flanked the front door.

He'd known she was living back here, near the newly constructed school, but he hadn't let himself think about it. But knowing something and seeing it were two different things. It was difficult to accept that she, pampered Frasier heiress, now lived in this primitive house, miles from the nearest neighbor.

He lifted the lantern from the buggy hook and smashed the guilt. He had no reason to feel guilty. He'd done nothing wrong.

And yet he knew she didn't belong here. She'd never survive a winter here. What did she know of hardship? What skills did she have to cope with Montana's rugged valley and vast wilderness?

He offered her his arm. She looked up at him, her dark gaze troubled.

"Take my arm." He gritted and, after a moment's hesitation, she did. He felt her gloved hand on his forearm and the light pressure of her hand seemed to sink all the way through the thick leather of his coat.

His guilt and unease spread, becoming an ache in his chest. If she did survive the winter, she'd never be the same.

Her fingers and hands would chap and crack from the harsh soaps and constant cold. She'd suffer windburn, and her face would sting every time she stepped outside. Come summer, the rawness would heal, but her complexion would never be the same, the delicate ivory permanently rough and red.

She didn't know any of this yet. She would learn the hard way in time.

He wished she'd found a job somewhere else. She was too isolated and vulnerable in this place. A half-dozen different dangers came to mind—animals, travelers, gamblers, drunkards, miners.

"Do you have a rifle?" he asked roughly.

For a split-second her grip tightened. "No."

"What do you use for protection?"

"I have a derringer. My father gave it to me before my last trip abroad." She glanced up, her brown eyes briefly searching his. "I understand it's a very good gun."

"Have you ever used it?"

"When I first received it. Father had me practice loading and shooting, but it's been awhile. Do you think I should practice again?"

"Yes, I do." He would have said more but her heel stuck in a muddy patch and he waited while she gathered her hem higher and extracted her foot.

"Then I will," she answered, once she'd worked her shoe free. "Thank you for the reminder."

He had to bite his tongue when she paused again to draw

her heavy gown up to keep it from trailing in the mud. And then he couldn't remain silent any longer. "Is it always this soggy?"

She dropped his arm to use both hands to lift her skirt higher, allowing her to take longer steps. "We're near the creek, which is good for fresh water, but it does tend to turn much of the field into a bog."

"What about mosquitos?"

"Plenty of those this summer."

"Any flooding?"

"Not since I've been here, and I've been told the creek isn't the issue. It's the Yellowstone in June." She darted another look up at him. "But June is months from now, so there is plenty of time to come up with a plan should the river flood."

He said nothing, not reassured.

She sighed. "I've a new house, and I'm grateful it's solid and structurally sound. The door is heavy. The windows don't rattle. I'm quite comfortable, I promise."

Sinclair nearly rolled his eyes. There was no way she was comfortable, but it was late, and they were both tired, and it was time he returned home to feed and water his livestock.

The lantern spilled light onto the small covered porch as they climbed the two wooden steps, shoes thudding on the boards.

She dropped her heavy skirts and opened the door before turning to face him. "Thank you for seeing me home." Her beautiful face tilted up, her dark eyes luminous in the lantern's golden light. "You've always been good to me." She hesitated. "Thank you for being my friend even when I don't deserve the kindness."

"Every human being deserves kindness."

"You know what I'm saying."

"The scriptures teach us to forgive."

"Does that mean you've forgiven me?"

"No. But I will. One day."

"Thank you." Her lips quivered. "Good night."

"Good night," he answered gruffly, his fingers tightening around the lantern handle to keep himself from reaching for her, touching her, tracing the elegant curve of her cheek, the arch of her eyebrow, the firmness of her small chin. It wasn't just her beauty he'd missed. He missed *her*.

He missed her laugh and the way the light danced in her eyes when she smiled. He missed the twitch of her lips when she was amused, and how her jaw firmed when she was angry. She was beautiful and fierce and fragile. Everything he'd ever wanted. Everything he thought he needed. And, even though years had passed, he still responded to her.

During the drive home tonight, her warmth and scent had teased him. He'd fought the urge to draw her closer and, when the buggy hit a rock or pothole and she'd spill sideways, her shoulder and hip brushing his, he'd want to hold her there, next to him. Instead, he'd hold his breath, fingers tightening on the leather reins and remind himself that she wasn't honest. That she wasn't true. He had to constantly remind himself that she wasn't his McKenna, nor had she ever been.

That would kill his desire for a little bit.

Until the next time they were jostled and she was thrown against him.

Sinclair was just about to climb up into his buggy when he glanced back at the cabin. It was still dark, no light yet shining inside, or curl of smoke coming from the chimney.

He hesitated, watching the chimney more closely.

Was she all right?

Had he allowed her to walk into a cabin that wasn't empty?

A gentleman would have entered the cabin first, checking the interior, ensuring that all was as it should be. Why had he left her, without knowing she was safe?

Sinclair turned around, sprinting across the filed. He crossed the porch in one swift step, and shoved at her door. The heavy door hadn't been locked yet and crashed open. McKenna let out a cry.

"McKenna?" He flashed the lantern around the dark room, trying to find her.

"What's wrong?"

He turned to the right, the light falling on her where she sat at a small table pushed up against the wall. Her eyes shone, overly bright. She'd either been crying, or trying not to cry, and he felt another pinch in his chest. "Why are you sitting in the dark?"

She tried to rise but sank back down onto her stool. "Is that why you broke down my door? Because it's dark in here?" Her voice cracked. "Sin, you scared me half to death!"

"I didn't break your door. It just banged loudly."

"You better not have broken it—"

"It's not broken." He held the lantern up, the yellow light streaming, revealing the simple bed, the stacked trunks serving as a wardrobe, and then the table and chair where McKenna sat now.

There wasn't much else, and the interior was Spartan but clean. The only hint of luxury was the thick quilt on the log bed, the large squares a mix of jeweled velvets and black wool, as if she'd taken her old dresses and coats and torn them apart. Perhaps she had. "Why is your fire not lit?" he asked.

She rose, reaching for the ribbons beneath her chin. "I didn't trust leaving it burning while I was gone."

"It'd be safe in your stove."

"I don't have one yet," she answered carelessly, untying the bow, and then easing off her bonnet. As she placed her bonnet on the table, she gestured to her fireplace filled with iron hooks and a tripod. "But I'm managing as you can see."

"You're cooking over the fire?" he asked incredulously.

Years ago, when his mother and father had first married, his mother had used their hearth as both stove and source of heat, but that was twenty-five years ago. He couldn't imagine her preparing meals without her beloved cast iron range.

"It's been an adventure," she said. "Some recipes are more successful than others."

It boggled his mind that McKenna was living like a starving immigrant. "Ridiculous. You should have a stove. I'll speak to—"

"Please don't. I had the one they were going to install here, put into the school so the children can stay warm when the weather changes. I want the classroom to be comfortable. They won't learn if they're miserable."

"They built a school without a proper stove?"

"There was one, but it was small, and I was worried about the cold. I would rather be able to keep the children safe, should there be another storm like last year's." Her voice was less steady. "This way I could keep them with me. Not have to send them home."

"That was an anomaly, one of the worst storms in history."

"But hundreds of people died last year, most of them children."

"And a dozen teachers."

"Not that many I think but, yes, teachers died, too, so you understand my concern."

"I appreciate your commitment to the children, but if you freeze to death in your cabin, you'll be of no use to anyone." His hard jaw eased. "If you won't let me speak to the school board, will you allow me to purchase a stove on your behalf—"

"Sin. *Please.*" Her voice dropped, deepening. "It's not… proper. It's not a gift I can accept."

"But I'm not giving it to you. It's for the house. It'll stay here with the house for future teachers long after you're gone."

He could see she was struggling with the offer as she tugged off her left glove. Her hands weren't steady, her voice wasn't steady, and she'd been fighting tears when he barged in.

She wasn't happy, and she could say she was fine, but he knew better. He knew this wasn't the life for her, and if he cared for her—which he did—then he'd get her out of Paradise Valley and back into society.

She needed society. She needed people. She wasn't cut out for the grueling winters and intense isolation.

"I don't want people to talk," she said hoarsely. "I can struggle with cooking better than I can the alienation." Her brow creased as she worked at her right glove. "The isolation has been the worst. I try not to think about it. I'm aware of my role in this. But I do need people to one day… forgive… me. And they won't, not if they think you're buying me things, or giving me gifts." The glove came off and she looked up at him, her eyes meeting his, her expression earnest. "Does that make sense?"

He swallowed hard, counting to five, and then ten. She'd just validated everything he'd been thinking. She couldn't stay here. She didn't belong here. He had to do something about this.

He needed to find her a rich man who could give her the life she wanted. Men became millionaires in the mines, whether here or in Nevada or California. These newly wealthy men would want a beautiful wife, and her past wouldn't trouble them. They'd take her west to San Francisco and build her a mansion on Nob Hill and she'd be the jewel of the city's crown.

It was where she belonged. It was the life she was best suited for. He knew without question she'd be happier there then in the middle of wilderness.

But until then, she was here, and in need of a practical education.

Spotting her kerosene lantern on the mantle, he crossed the floor, searched through the small knickknacks on the mantle for the matches, and found the small tin tucked behind the lantern.

He struck the match and lit the lantern for her. "You don't think they will talk now?" He turned to face her. "After I've taken you home?"

She grew still. "Do you think anyone knows?"

"I don't know, but all it takes is one person looking out the window and the gossip begins."

"You should have said something before we left the Brambles."

"It crossed my mind but I was more concerned about

your physical safety at that point of time."

"You're awfully preoccupied about my safety."

"I am. I don't think you should be out here. I'm disgusted that the school board hired you—"

"Disgusted?"

"Have you seen the women in this valley? They are thin and worn, weathered from work and cold. This is not the life for you. You were not raised on the plains or the prairie. You haven't been taught how to hunt or cook, sew or do laundry."

"I can do needlework."

"Embroidery."

"I've repaired my gowns, Sinclair. I can replace buttons and stitch a hem. It takes a needle and thread and a little bit of patience, which clearly you do not have."

"Were there no teaching positions in St. Louis? You couldn't go to Denver? Why choose a school that's in the middle of nowhere? You don't have a clue how to survive here."

"It's none of your business. I'm not your responsibility, or your problem, and it might surprise you to discover that I have a brain, and it's a very good one. I'm fully aware of the dangers living out here. No one has to tell me about wild animals as I hear them every night when I'm in bed. I've lived in the city and I've seen men at their worst—raucous and aggressive, and lecherous from drink. I know what bad men do. I am in my current situation because of a man…

and I'm not talking about the man who compromised me, but the man who fathered me. I understand that he was disappointed in me. I am disappointed in me. But turning his back on me? Putting me on the streets?" She shook her head, furious, and indignant. "That is no way to handle a problem, much less a member of your family. And you're not helping, either."

She pointed to the door. "So go, and stop frightening me with all the horrible things that could happen. Yes, this is new for me. Yes, it's intimidating. But I am going to make this work. I am going to prove everyone—including you— wrong. Good night."

SHIVERING, MCKENNA CLIMBED into bed, covers pulled up to her chin. Her father loved technology and every new innovation had found its way into his mines and his homes. She'd grown up with light and warmth and what she wouldn't give to have gas and electricity here, never mind plumbing.

What she wouldn't give for running water and a proper toilet. Her father had the most lovely copper tanks and porcelain bowls installed in the bathrooms at the house on Fifth Avenue. She'd her very own suite there—a sitting room, a bedroom, and an adjacent bathroom with endless hot water for long luxurious soaks in the gorgeous claw-footed tub. She hadn't appreciated those hot baths, and beautiful sinks and modern toilets until now. She hadn't appreciated a lot of things until now.

Exhaling, McKenna drew her covers higher and nestled into her pillow, trying to relax, but everything inside of her was still a knotted mess.

Driving home with Sinclair had made her want to weep. Being near him had been bewildering—at times, wonderful, at others, terrible, and even now it struck her as more bitter than sweet.

She'd forgotten his impact, and how intensely he made her feel. She'd met him in primary school, when they were both students at the new, small public school in downtown Butte. He was four years older so they weren't friends, but he had a sister her age, Johanna, and she and Johanna didn't play together, but they knew each other, and sometimes at recess or lunch, McKenna would join Johanna and the other girls at the edge of the field to watch the older boys play football and baseball. Johanna was very proud that her big brother Sinclair was the best athlete at their school. He was so good that one of the male teachers told Mrs. Douglas that Sinclair should try to travel to Chicago and meet with the coaches putting together those new professional teams. Johanna told the little girls listening that her mother let the teacher have it, because Sinclair was needed at home and the teacher wasn't to encourage her only son to go chasing after impractical dreams. Even though Mrs. Douglas squashed the teacher, all the girls were impressed by the notion that

Sinclair was that good.

Sinclair *was* that good.

Eyes closed, McKenna scooted lower beneath her covers, sleepy, dreamy. From the time she was just a girl, Sinclair had fascinated McKenna, and not just because he was an exceptional athlete, but he was genuinely kind and one of the most handsome boys at their school, which made him popular. It was impossible not to respond to him, which was probably why he was promoted every year into the next grade even though he couldn't read. The teachers and principal just looked the other way, not wanting to penalize Sinclair when he showed up every day with his winning smile, and put in the effort, and was respectful to everyone.

But that all changed when McKenna was in sixth grade. Their school got a new principal, and the principal wasn't about to let students advance if they couldn't pass basic subjects, and Sinclair was one of the students the principal held up as examples of Butte's failed education.

To make his point, he assigned younger students to tutor the older ones, and McKenna, an outstanding student, was assigned to Sinclair to help improve his reading.

"I'm sorry," McKenna had whispered when Sinclair sat down in her classroom, forced to cram his big body into a desk for eleven year olds.

"Not your fault," he'd answered. "Besides, I'd rather it be you than someone else. Johanna says you are always helping everyone with hard subjects, so at least I know you're a good teacher."

She'd opened the books the principal had given her for their first lesson. It was a reading primer that the "babies" used in Kindergarten and first grade. She was mortified that she was to make Sinclair read this out loud, to her. She understood the principal was making a point, shaming Sinclair publically for being a dunce.

But he wasn't a dunce. He was the hero of the whole school.

McKenna remembered how her eyes had filled with tears as he slowly, carefully read the childish story about a six-year-old boy and his dog, and how the dog followed the boy to school every day.

Reading wasn't easy for Sinclair, but he got through that first juvenile story without mistakes. Tomorrow he would return to her to read the next story to her, and so on and so on until he had proven himself.

She had hated those lessons, hating it even more when Mr. Betts entered the class to stand behind them as Sinclair read aloud, because that was when he'd get nervous, and struggle, and then Mr. Betts would ridicule him before the entire class.

Four months later, Sinclair's father died in the mines, and he abruptly left school.

McKenna remembered almost being happy for him because he didn't have to endure Mr. Betts' ridicule any longer.

But she had also missed him, and she'd wanted to ask

Johanna about him, but she felt guilty because Mr. Douglas was dead, and he'd died from something in her father's mine, and now Sinclair was going to work in the same copper mine, too.

A month after he'd left school, Johanna had given her a note from Sinclair asking if McKenna had any books that he could maybe read, because Mr. Betts was right. Only dunces couldn't read and he wasn't a dunce.

McKenna had spent a whole day trying to figure out what book to send to him and she ended up taking the popular Horatio Alger novel, *Ragged Dick*, off her father's shelf in the library. She'd wrapped it up in one of her handkerchiefs and taken it to school and asked Johanna to give it to Sinclair.

She'd heard nothing from him for months and then the book came back wrapped in brown paper with a note, thanking her and asking if there was maybe another Alger novel he could read.

She'd sent the second book in the series, *Fame and Fortune*, in another of her handkerchiefs along with a note asking him to be careful in his work because she knew the mines were dangerous.

He'd answered with a simple note. *McKenna, Thank you for your concern. I work hard and try to be safe. Your friend, Sin Douglas*

Months passed, and the book came back. He'd turned seventeen and she was thirteen and he was ready for another story, if she had one she could recommend. She sent the third Alger on her father's shelf, *Rough and Ready*.

It was the last of the Alger novels in her father's library and she was thinking she might need to persuade him to order another one when the book came back after just a few weeks. *McKenna, thank you for sending the book but I think I've had enough Alger. Your friend, Sin*

She had been so distressed by the note, and she wrote him immediately, asking if she could please send something else.

He'd answered a week later. *I am too tired to read, but I remain your friend. Sin*

She did not see him, or hear from him, for over a year. By then she was fourteen and a freshman in high school, and participating in the Christmas choral recital. Johanna had been in the December recital, too. Parents and families filled the school. Sinclair was one of them, attending the evening recital with his mother.

McKenna had spotted him in the folding chairs long before Johanna nudged her to point him out. How could one not see Sinclair when he was so fair and stood a full head taller than anyone else?

At eighteen, he didn't just look like a man, he'd become a man. She'd felt something shift in her that night. Just looking at him made her realize how much she'd missed him, and how very glad she was to see him tonight.

After the concert she'd wanted to speak to him but there

was no way to reach him, not when her father and mother swept her and Mary out quickly, not wanting to linger amongst the other families.

But as she was hurried out the doors she'd spotted him outside, off to one side, and she caught his eye, and she hadn't been able to look away, despite the jostling and conversation around her.

She'd only wanted to look at him.

She'd wanted to remember him.

He was the most handsome boy she'd ever seen, with his light hair and dark blue eyes, and yet she also knew that at eighteen he wasn't a boy, but a man, except in her heart, he was *her* boy. She didn't know when it happened, or how it happened, but at fourteen, McKenna couldn't imagine ever wanting any one but him.

CHAPTER FIVE

SINCLAIR WAS UP early Sunday for chores. It was one of those mornings where it felt good to be outside in the crisp morning, watching the sun rise over the mountains, revealing a delicate blue sky with wispy layers of clouds. The sunrise turned the snowy peak of Emigrant Mountain pink and the gold aspens on the valley floor a liquid copper.

Even as a boy he'd loved being outside. All he ever wanted to do was run and move. Going to work underground at fifteen and a half had almost killed him.

But he survived it, and he'd learned to appreciate each day as a gift. He was grateful, too, that he could provide for his mother, and that he'd had the ability to help his sister start her own business. He never wanted his family dependent on anyone again.

Returning to the house, he bathed and changed into clean clothes before saddling his horse to ride into Marietta for Sunday supper with his mother and sister. He normally enjoyed the weekly family meal, but today the focus would be on yesterday's party at the Brambles. Neither his sister nor mother had been invited to the party. They were liked well enough in town, but weren't considered part of Marietta society. He'd hope to change that by building them a handsome house on Bramble Lane, but his sister convinced their mother that it was better to have a bigger nest egg, than invitations to social events.

Even five years after moving to the area, Sinclair still had no interest in Marietta events and functions. He hadn't come to Crawford County to make friends, and he wasn't interested in any of the women. No, he arrived with two goals—claim land and establish Frasier's mine, hoping this mountain would be as good as the one in Butte.

It had taken nine months before the Frasier mine began producing and, just like in Butte, it was grueling work in miserable, suffocating conditions. As the manager, he didn't have to go underground daily. He could have left the inspections to others, but he was the most experienced man on the jobsite, and he personally wanted to ensure the safety of his men as well as measure daily progress.

After fifteen years of working for Patrick Frasier, Sinclair walked off the job in July following a tragedy that did not have to happen.

He'd warned Frasier countless times there were serious problems at the mine, citing the dangerous technology, unskilled labor, and excessive production quota. Sinclair had even implemented measures to improve conditions—better wages to attract higher caliber workers, as well as more training for the workers—but when the safety measures cut into profit, Frasier rejected them. The mine accident happened just five weeks later.

The accident enraged Sinclair, the loss of life was avoidable, and unacceptable. He'd warned Frasier. Hell, he'd warned everyone. It hadn't mattered. Sinclair was done. He refused to be party to abuse and negligence.

Leaving his property, Sinclair spurred his horse into a canter. It felt good to move. After last night's agonizing ride with McKenna, he relished the wind at his back and the sunlight dappling the road.

When he passed the narrow dirt turnoff leading to the school and McKenna's cabin, he briefly glanced to the right, thinking of her, but not thinking of her.

She'd been on his mind all morning. He wasn't going to give her the entire day. She was content with her work and settled in her home. He should be happy. *Relieved.*

He'd done his duty, seeing her home last night, and he'd tried to help her—help she clearly didn't want—so he could stop worrying about her. They'd survived their first encounter, and even though it was uncomfortable, they'd survive future encounters. There was nothing more that needed to be done. And last night's conversation made him understand there was no going back, either. The past was the past. Their relationship had been one of children, and neither of them was innocent anymore. He could move on, *finally.*

He reached town in half the time it'd taken him last night with the buggy. He was glad he'd chosen to ride. The exercise calmed him, easing some of the tension inside, giving him a chance to mentally prepare for all the questions his sister would have about McKenna. He was sure there would be plenty.

He was right.

Johanna couldn't even wait for the meal to end before she demanded a full account of the Brambles' revels. She'd made dresses for a number of the women attending and asked what everyone wore, wanting to know who was the most fashionable, and if Mrs. Bramble wore her blue silk or the handsome chocolate velvet gown.

Sinclair shook his head. "I don't remember what Mrs. Bramble wore. It might have been the navy or the brown. My overall impression was that she looked handsome."

"I would hope it wasn't the navy, because Mrs. Wettstein was going to wear navy, too. But hers was a brocade."

"I don't believe I know Mrs. Wettstein, and I don't recall brocade."

"What about Hattie Harris, was she wearing purple? She loves purple even though its not the right color for her."

"I did see Miss Harris, and I do believe she was wearing purple."

"Did she look sickly?"

He grinned at his sister. "No, she did not. But her mother was keeping her close. I think Miss Harris would enjoy a little more freedom."

"Indeed she would. Mrs. Harris is quote formidable."

Johanna folded her white linen napkin. "And what about Miss Frasier? Did she wear the saffron gown, or the blush velvet with lace?"

"Saffron," he answered without thinking, and then he saw Johanna's triumphant expression and realized his sister had deliberately trapped him. Johanna was too clever for her own good. "Yes, she was there."

"You spoke to her?"

"It would have been rude not to."

"Was she as entitled as ever?"

His amusement vanished. He took his time answering, lifting his cup, and sipping his coffee. It was stronger than usual, thank goodness. His mother was a tea drinker and didn't understand that good coffee had to be robust.

Johanna tapped her spoon to her saucer to get his attention. "Fine. Don't answer. I know the answer already."

"She did nothing to hurt you, Johanna—"

"Not true, Sin. She used me to get close to you. For years."

"You were friends in school from an early age."

"We were classmates, but not friends, not until she decided she fancied you, and then it was 'Johanna, this, and Johanna that', and suddenly she wanted to sit with me at lunch, and walk with me at recess. I was a convenient friend, nothing more."

"You admired her, Jo, and you were pleased that someone like McKenna wanted to be friends with you. None of the other girls from Dublin Gulch were invited to the Frasiers."

"I was only invited a few times, and the invitations stopped when Mr. Frasier found out who I was."

"And yet that didn't stop you from wearing her hand-me-downs, or taking apart the dresses to see how they were constructed."

"I have pride, but I'm not a fool."

He shrugged and glanced over to his mother who'd been sitting quietly, her fingers nervously tracing the pattern of lace in the tablecloth. "What's the matter, mam? Are you upset, too?"

Her gray head bobbed. "We should not have encouraged you. She was never right for you."

"We never encouraged, Sinclair," Johanna cried, outraged. "*She* did. She wrote you those letters and I was forced to carry them back and forth—"

"I wrote her first, Jo, and I *asked* you to carry the letters. I asked you to be kind to her for me, for my sake."

"I wish I hadn't done it," Johanna snapped, angrily stacking dishes, making them clatter. "She never deserved you. She never deserved us. We treated her like a princess, too. Like royalty. Right, mum?"

Mrs. Douglas held up her hands. "I don't wish to quarrel with Sinclair. It's Sunday, and he's a man. He's entitled to make his choices."

Johanna dropped a fork onto the china. "Terrible choices! Her father would never have approved his suit. Mr. Patrick Frasier wasn't about to let an Irish miner's son marry his fancy daughter—"

"Enough," Sin growled, patience shot. "Leave her alone."

"And you're still protecting her!"

"I was well aware that I would never be her father's choice and I wouldn't be where I am now, if it hadn't been for Mr. Patrick Frasier. You wouldn't be here, either, with your own dress shop without his help. He gave me the opportunity—"

"And you, my boy, made the most of it," Mrs. Douglas interjected quietly. "It was you that did the work. It killed your father but you survived, and you're out, and you're never going back."

Sinclair smiled faintly. "I'm done with Frasier mines. I promise you that."

Mrs. Douglas smiled back. "Good."

"Now just promise me you're done with the Frasier girl," Johanna said, rising with the dishes.

The pressure in his chest returned. "There is no going back, Johanna, we all know that."

"I hope not," his sister answered, sweeping to the sink.

Mrs. Douglas leaned towards her son. "I'm glad to hear, Sinclair. But does the Frasier girl know that?"

"The Frasier girl is a twenty-five-year old woman, Mother."

"Exactly. She has nothing to lose anymore. But you…

you're a different story. You have everything now. You're healthy. You're successful. You're respected. You don't need her. She can do nothing for you."

"Do you really despise her so much?"

"If you hadn't met her, you'd be married now, with children."

"There is plenty of time for me to have a family."

"I want grandchildren. I want to enjoy them while I can."

"You will."

"When?"

The corner of his mouth lifted. "Don't be pushy."

"You're almost thirty."

"*Mother.*"

Johanna returned to the table and refilled Sinclair's coffee. Steam wafted from the cup. "We just don't want to see you hurt," she said quietly.

"I understand, and I appreciate your concern, but I'm a man. I've never been coddled. Don't start now.

"Just remember you are someone, Sinclair Douglas. You don't need those Frasiers anymore!"

HIS MOTHER'S WORDS rang in Sinclair's head long after he'd left the lights of Marietta behind. *You don't need those Frasiers anymore...*

She was right, and wrong.

He didn't need them anymore, but apparently he was still drawn to one because McKenna had very much been on his mind throughout dinner.

But then, everything he'd done, everything he'd achieved had been for her.

He was successful because he'd needed to be successful... for her. How else could he approach her father? How else could he hope to marry her?

It had been backbreaking work, opening the new mine. Accidents and inclement weather slowed their progress, but finally, a year after production commenced, he was able to open up a savings account at one of the banks on Marietta's Main Street.

A year later, the mine was doing well, and he was profiting, so much so, that Patrick Frasier threatened to cut Sinclair's percentage in half. Fed up, Sinclair gave notice, letting Frasier know that the new mine three miles west wanted him for twice what Frasier was paying him. Frasier responded with a telegram filled with curse words and exclamation points, offering Sinclair twice what the rival mine owners were willing to pay him.

For the first time in his life, Sinclair Douglas was making real money, the kind of money that if invested properly would make him wealthy.

He sat down with Henry Bramble, told him what he was earning and what he'd so far saved and, with Henry's guidance, they laid out a plan, investing in opportunities across the country. Two failed, one broke even, and the fourth succeeded beyond his wildest dreams, turning him into a millionaire in less than two years.

The only one who knew his finances was Henry Bramble. He didn't even tell his family just how well he was doing. It was no one's business but his own, so whatever came in from his investments, was quietly reinvested again, with Sinclair living off his earnings from the mine.

During his fourth year in Marietta, he used his mine income to buy land, and then cattle, and eventually he built a house and outbuildings on his property, working his property on the weekends during the year, and every evening during the summer months, taking advantage of the extra hours of daylight.

Maybe it was Henry Bramble's friendship that gave him entrance into Marietta society. He didn't know, or care, just as he didn't seek out approval. He knew who he was, and what he was, and as long as he stayed true to his values, he was happy.

And then came news of the scandal. Each headline worse than the last. McKenna Frasier had stumbled. McKenna Frasier had been exposed. McKenna Frasier was a fallen woman. And then, McKenna had been disinherited…

Those had been some of the worst weeks of his life.

Urging his horse to a canter, he breathed deeply, trying to slow the hard thudding of his pulse and ease the tightness in his chest that had been there ever since he'd heard she'd been hired for the Paradise Valley school.

He had been baffled by the knot in his chest, and he didn't understand it, but it seemed—*despite everything*—she still possessed a small part of him. She was part of his being, living in a corner of his heart, and he could try to hate her, but that would be like hating himself.

She was impossible.

Beyond maddening.

And maybe that was why he'd fallen in love with her in the first place.

MCKENNA WAS AT the table, wrapped up in layers of sweaters, writing letters to her friends back east, including a very long, chatty letter to Amelia Harris who loved McKenna's adventures and always wanted more stories, when a knock sounded at her door. She put down her pen and sat tall, glancing towards her windows. It was dark out, and she hadn't heard anyone approach.

"Who's there?" she called, rising.

"It's Sinclair."

The deep voice sent a shiver through her. She hadn't expected to see him again, at least, not so soon. She opened the door warily. "You startled me."

He entered the house, carrying a fabric wrapped bundle. "Soda bread and butter," he said. "And a little bit of cake, too."

"You didn't make this."

"No, my mother."

"How kind of her. Thank you." McKenna accepted the bundle, and lifted it to her nose, breathing in the scent of freshly baked bread before placing the care package in her makeshift kitchen. "How is she?"

"Good." He glanced from her to the fireplace.

She followed his gaze. The fire wasn't burning well. She'd allowed the ashes to build up too much. "I have to clean it," she said. "I was going to do it once I finished the essays but the day escaped."

There was something in his expression that reminded her of last night, and how the rough road would jostle her and she'd fall against him. He had the same pained look tonight, his handsome features hard, his expression remote.

"It's a lot of work for one person," he said.

"Far more than I anticipated," she admitted.

He opened his mouth to say something but changed his mind. He walked the length of her house, floorboards squeaking beneath his heavy boots. "It's drafty," he said after he'd crossed from one end to the other, and back.

"I'm thinking of turning some of my evening gowns into curtains."

He glanced towards her bed with the thick quilt of jeweled velvet and black wool. "It looks like some of them have already met their fate."

"Mr. Worth would be aghast."

The corner of his mouth lifted, and his expression softened a fraction as his blue eyes rested on her and then his smile faded and he looked at her as if he didn't know her. Or, if he knew her, he didn't like her.

It was brutal.

A lump filled her throat and her fingers curled into her palms.

She couldn't cry. She wouldn't. She'd cried herself sick after her father disowned her last May and she'd promised herself she wouldn't cry again. There was no point in crying. She'd brought this on herself. She had no one to blame.

"Who was he?" Sinclair's deep voice shattered the silence. "Why did you love him?"

"I didn't," she whispered, caught off guard.

"Then why the scandal if he wasn't your lover?"

"I couldn't control the gossip," she said faintly, sick at heart, and sick to her stomach.

"Newspaper headlines don't help."

"I shouldn't have trusted him—" She broke off, shook her head. "No, I can't blame him. I can only blame myself, because I thought I could manage him. I thought I could manage the situation."

"Just as you managed me."

"*No.*" She saw Sinclair's mouth compress, his expression scornful. "I didn't manage you. It wasn't like that... I never meant to lead you on—"

"But you did. And you thought you could lead him,

too."

"No."

"You thought he would fall at your heel and be obedient."

She exhaled hard, nauseated. "You are twisting everything. You are taking what we had—"

"Miss Frasier, we had nothing." His deep voice was brutally hard. "But you and Mr. Clark, you had something. Maybe it wasn't an affair of the heart, but from all reports, he most definitely had you."

"That's quite enough, *Mr. Douglas.*"

"Is that your very best set down? Should I roll over now and give up? I think not. Tell me about your Jeremy Bernard Clark. Why was he the one?"

She shouldn't have been surprised that he knew Bernard's name, but it still was a shock to hear his name on Sinclair's lips. "He wasn't the one. He most definitely wasn't the *one*. He just…"

"What?"

"Was smart enough to identify my weaknesses, and then exploit them." She felt Sinclair's quick narrowed glance. Her shoulders shifted. "I'm proud. I'm stubborn. I crave freedom and independence."

Sinclair said nothing and she quietly added, "I was never compromised the way you think, but I ignored propriety, I ignored common sense, going places with him that I shouldn't have gone, being seen late at night without a chaperone. It was scandalous behavior and, in my heart, I knew it."

"And you didn't care?"

"I don't know. I can barely remember that girl, but in hindsight, I should have cared more." She rubbed the fringe of her sweater between her fingers. "I should have listened to those who tried to save me before it was too late."

"People did speak to you?"

She nodded once.

"Were they people you trusted?"

"Yes. No. I thought they were very stuffy and old-fashioned. I thought because I was educated and modern that I could do things differently, and Sinclair, it was exciting. For a few weeks there I felt... free."

"Where did Mr. Clark take you?"

"Anywhere. Everywhere. It was like a game. Sneaking out late at night, going to bawdy theatres, exploring Central Park."

He shot her a swift look, his expression disapproving. "And that was worth ruining yourself for?"

For a long moment, she couldn't speak. She didn't want to answer, and yet she couldn't lie to him. She didn't want to lie to him. "I didn't think it would ruin me."

"Being seen with an improper man late at night?

This time she didn't answer.

"McKenna."

She looked at him.

"Tell me."

"I thought I was above the rules."

"*What*? How?"

She shrugged and laughed, because it was either that or shrivel with shame. "Oh, Sinclair, you know me. I am McKenna Frasier. I thought the rules didn't pertain to me."

He muttered something rough beneath his breath. "If he had been a gentleman he would have protected you, as I have tried to protect you."

"I know," she said.

"And you liked this? That he wasn't a gentleman? You liked that he took advantage of you?"

"I wasn't thinking. Not in the beginning. He was handsome and charming and I enjoyed his company immensely."

"What did you enjoy?"

"He wasn't so stiff, and he wasn't dull. He made me laugh. He told jokes and went out his way to entertain me."

"And he made love to you."

She winced at his tone, feeling increasingly defensive. "He made me feel beautiful."

"You *are* beautiful."

It wasn't a compliment the way he said it. It was more like a slap. She flushed, fingers tangling in the yarn. "But desirable... like there was no one else like me."

"Because there *was* no one else like you, McKenna."

McKenna bit into her lower lip, digging into the softness to keep from making a sound. He'd said *was*.

It didn't matter. None of it mattered. What was done was done and she couldn't go back. There was no point trying to defend herself, either, because she had known her behavior was bordering on scandalous, and she'd known deep down that if she was discovered, it wouldn't be good, that her father would be angry. And yet she'd thought she could manage Father. She'd tease him, reminding him that she was like him—strong willed and stubborn and incorrigible. And that might have been okay, if Bernard had been a different man, with different intentions.

"Am I supposed to be sympathetic?" he asked, his voice rough and hard.

"No."

"And you really didn't think there would be consequences?"

"It was all... silly. Frivolous. I had no idea Mr. Clark had an agenda. Now I realize I should have known. I should have realized he wasn't with me because he liked me, but rather I was the means to an end."

"What did he want?"

"Money. Power. A piece of my father's company." She hesitated. "He compromised me, certain my father would reward him with some kind of settlement, or dowry. I refused to marry him and Father was outraged, not just because I wouldn't marry Mr. Clark, but because Mr. Clark dared threaten my father, revealing all to the scandal sheets."

"And he did."

"Oh, yes, he did."

"Your father is so rich he could have easily bought Mr. Clark's silence."

"Easily, but you know my father. You don't dictate to Patrick Frasier, and God help the man that blackmails him. Livid, Father ran him out of town, and Mr. Clark went straight to the press."

"Where is Mr. Clark today?"

"I don't know. California? Alaska? The Continent? I'm sure he has a new plan, and is doing his best to marry another heiress, or swindle another millionaire."

"I can't imagine your father being happy to see you married to a swindler."

"He would have hated it. I am certain he would have disowned me either way. Father cannot abide the man who wants wealth without having to work for it, or respect without earning it."

Sinclair shook his head, disgusted. "It's late. I have to go."

CHAPTER SIX

McKENNA HELD HER breath for a long minute after Sinclair left, and then she forced herself to action.

It's better this way. She locked the door behind him. He knows the truth. He knows the whole story.

And it was better for him to know, she insisted when her eyes burned, hot and gritty. It was better for him to know who she was, and just how silly, and shallow, and vain, she'd become.

But doing the right thing didn't mean she was comfortable with what she'd told him because, in her heart, she was more than silly and shallow and frivolous. What she hadn't told him was that she'd disagreed with all the rules imposed by society. She'd found them narrow and confining and hypocritical, as well. Men could travel where they pleased, and how they pleased, without anyone thinking anything of it. But if a young woman went out without the right companion, she was loose. Immoral.

Even if she was a virgin and was careful with her virtue.

The facts didn't matter.

It was enough that slander could ruin a woman, because

her purity was the most important thing about her.

And McKenna didn't even know how to defend herself when the attacks began, because, yes, Mr. Clark had kissed her, and touched her inappropriately. But he hadn't disrobed her, nor had she lain with him, even though he'd tried. He'd become quite nasty, too, when she refused him. She hadn't ever meant for things to get that far, but he seemed to be an expert at seduction and she apparently was too easily seduced.

That was why she didn't know how to protest her innocence. She wasn't entirely innocent. She'd played a part in her disgrace, having slipped out of her home at an hour when single ladies didn't travel about town to attend a risqué show at an equally risqué theatre. She'd had two more glasses of champagne than she should have, and permitted him to touch her in public.

No, of course she shouldn't have allowed his wandering hand to touch her back, her shoulder, her waist. But her head had been fuzzy from the bubbles and fizz, and as he leaned close to kiss her, his lips lingering on hers, she'd felt daring and alive. Half of the fun had been feeling as if she was doing something wicked and forbidden. Burlesque—also known as extravaganzas in her circle—wasn't for ladies. Good women didn't attend raunchy shows where barely clothed female performers danced and sang, placing them just one step above prostitutes.

It was a good thing she'd enjoyed the shows and the

champagne because attending the extravaganzas with a man of questionable reputation ruined hers.

In the end, it didn't matter that she was still a virgin. What mattered to those who paid attention to scandal sheets and gossip rags—never mind society dragons—was that McKenna Frasier had proven herself to be a most unfortunate woman, a woman of lax morals and questionable virtue. Society washed their hands of her, forcing her out of New York.

It was almost comical how fast she fell from grace.

McKenna was still wrestling with the consequences of her shame when she crossed the frosty field to the school house the next morning, her teeth chattering from the cold. After lighting the fire in the stoves, she went to the big blackboard at the front of the classroom and began to write out the morning's lesson, and as the chalk squeaked across the board, she suddenly pictured a different classroom in a different school.

Her school in Butte had been large, and there were dozens of students in her classes, and yet the only two she remembered was Sinclair and Johanna.

McKenna left the chalkboard and went to her desk and took out her lesson plan book and yet she couldn't focus on the work in front of her. All she could see was Butte and suddenly she was there, remembering how Johanna suddenly left school abruptly, just like Sinclair did.

"I'm leaving school," Johanna announced.

McKenna followed Johanna from the classroom to the hall.
"What? Why? There are only six weeks left until the year ends.
Don't leave now!"

"I've been hired at Blum's as a shop girl. I'll be helping ladies with their purchases in the women's department, and they
need me to start immediately," Johanna answered.

"There will be other jobs—"

"Says who? And will they be at Blum's? I love fashion and I
know the dresses are ready-made, but it's a chance to do what I
enjoy. And I don't enjoy studying. I hate school."

"But you're smart, Johanna, and you could do so much more
with a high school education."

"I don't think so. Not for someone like me. And Sinclair
agrees with me. Why shouldn't I help with expenses? It's not fair
that he has to support all of us."

"Does your brother know that you're brilliant at math?"

"He does. That's why he thinks I should take the position. If
I worked hard I could eventually get promoted, maybe even run
the women's department." She smiled at McKenna. "You know,
not everyone loves reading and writing essays as much as you
do."

"I don't love reading and writing essays." She wrinkled her
nose "I mean, I do love reading but I'd rather read more novels
and a lot less history."

"Well, you must not mind if you want to go to college back
east. But I'm ready to do something else, and I'd far rather help
women select dresses and everything else. I know you'd never
wear ready-made dresses, but maybe you need a pair of stockings

or gloves?"

"Maybe," McKenna answered unconvincingly.

"You are such a snob!"

"I'm not."

"You are, or you'd happily come to Blum's so I could wait on you."

"Do you get a commission?"

"Oh, I don't know. But if I do, you'll have to order a dozen stockings?"

"Do I have to wear them?"

"You are such a little princess!"

"I'm sorry. Forgive me."

"Only if you say yes to supper on Sunday. Sinclair and I will walk to collect you, or if you think it's too far, he can rent a buggy."

"My mother hosts these music afternoons on Sunday, but I hate them and I want to come to dinner. I'll figure it out."

"Oh, and he wouldn't want me saying anything, but it's Sinclair's birthday."

Nothing would keep McKenna from going now.

The Douglas' lived in a small wood-framed house on Ana-conda Road in Dublin Gulch where the roofs of each residence nearly touched. But once inside the modest home, it was clear from the best dishes on the linen covered table that Mrs. Douglas had gone to great lengths to impress McKenna.

McKenna had brought gifts with her—potted African violets for Mrs. Douglas, chocolates for the family, and a burlap bag of mixed nuts for Sinclair. They ate supper almost immediately, sitting down to baked ham, mashed potatoes, and roast cauli-flower and root vegetables.

Johanna and McKenna carried the conversation with Mrs. Douglas interjecting only now and then with a soft question or comment. Sinclair, for his part, just listened, his expression revealing little, and yet more than once, McKenna glanced at him only to find him watching her intently.

It was dizzying to be subjected to such scrutiny. The year had changed him. Twelve months of laboring in the mines had added muscle to his frame and maturity to his face. His hair was still a thick, dark blond, but there was a burning intensity in his blue eyes that hadn't been there before. He looked at McKenna as if he memorizing her, aware that it was unlikely he'd ever seen her again.

"You can't make me sad today," she whispered, heart thumping. "Not on your birthday."

"I think this must be my favorite birthday."

For a moment she couldn't speak, hot emotion filling her. "Your mother was very kind to include me today."

"She was quite anxious to not offend you in any way."

"She couldn't possibly offend me. Everything was lovely. She's an excellent cook."

"I shall tell her you said so. That will please her greatly."

For a moment there was just silence and then McKenna blurted, "I hate that you work in the mine. It is quite danger-ous. Every day the newspapers are filled with tragic stories—"

"Don't read them."

"Is it really so unsafe?"

His broad shoulders shifted. *"I'm told that they're no worse here than the mines in England or Ireland."*

"Is it true that my father's mine is more dangerous than the others?"

"He's implementing new technology. The goal is to improve the working conditions."

"But it hasn't yet, has it?"

Sinclair hesitated. *"Technology fails, and there will always be human error."*

"And there is no way to eliminate human error?"

"With the right procedures and protocols it can be reduced, but eliminated? No."

Uneasy, she held her breath, trying to slow her jagged pulse. She couldn't imagine the world without him. She couldn't imagine her world without him. *"Is there no other work you can do?"*

"A man doesn't walk away from honest work and a regular paycheck."

"You could learn another trade—"

"Not here. I'd have to leave and I won't do that to my mother. She's buried a husband and five children. My sister and I are all she has left."

"She's lost five children?"

"Still births and the influenza." He leaned forward abruptly, and reached across the table as if to touch her but he drew back at the last second. *"But this is distressing you, and I do not want to do that. This has been a very good birthday. You've made me happy today. Thank you for coming."*

The earnestness in his deep voice made her eyes burn. "You will make me cry."

"Never."

"I'm about to cry now."

"You can't do that. My mother will be absolutely distraught if she brings in the cake and finds you weeping at her table." He smiled crookedly, but there was something besides laughter in his blue eyes, an emotion deeper and stronger, and it made her heart ache.

"I know I'm not supposed to pay you compliments since I'm not free to court you, but you look beautiful today," he added, and then he did extend his fingers, the tips grazing hers.

A shiver coursed through her.

She shouldn't touch him, shouldn't want to touch him and yet her fingers flexed, and she let her hand brush across his. His palm was thickly calloused and yet his skin was so warm and, when his fingers closed around hers, she felt a surge of energy all the way through her.

It went against all propriety, but this was how a man's hand should feel. Strong. Capable. Like Sinclair himself.

She loved him. It wasn't a question, or a game. He was her soul mate, her other half. There was no doubt in her mind. They would be together. It was just a matter of finishing school and then convincing her father that Sinclair was the right match.

After the birthday dinner, they didn't see each other often, but somehow, every few weeks, they did find a way to meet, if not at Blum's, where they'd walk and talk their way from one end of the department store to the other, then downtown riding the street car, and then they wouldn't talk, they'd just hold hands in secret, a coat or shopping bags hiding that they were touching.

The intensity of her feelings used to frighten her, as did the consuming nature of the attraction. She spent her nights worrying how to convince her father to accept Sinclair as a suitor, and then she worried that maybe Sinclair would not approach her father.

It was Sinclair who brought the topic up, just weeks before her high school graduation. "If I thought you were ready to marry, I'd approach your father next month, but you're not ready."

"You do want to marry me though, don't you?"

"I love you."

"Then promise me you'll wait for me. Promise me you won't marry anyone while I'm gone."

"What about you? Will you fall in love with someone in New York?"

"Never. I love you." She meant it, too. Her love burned within her. He had no idea how strongly he made her feel.

CHAPTER SEVEN

I T WAS A week to day since the Hallowe'en party at the
Brambles, and McKenna had visitors, and not just any
visitors, but Johanna and Mrs. Douglas.

McKenna had been cleaning her fireplace—a task she'd
put off for far too long—when she'd heard voices outside,
feminine voices, and she grabbed a cloth, scrubbed at her
soot-blackened hands, before opening her door.

"Johanna," she exclaimed, stepping out on to the porch,
shocked to see Sinclair's sister and mother on her doorstep.
"Mrs. Douglas. It's so nice to see you. Come in, come in."

She drew them into her home, suddenly nervous. She
gestured towards the fireplace. "I'm sorry I don't have a fire
lit. I thought since its mild today I would do a bit of housekeeping." McKenna knew she was talking too much but she
felt embarrassed to be caught in an old work dress with soot
on her hands and face. "Where should we sit? I haven't done
any entertaining yet. I have a stool and the rocking chair and
I can sit on the side of my bed."

"Don't fuss on our account," Mrs. Douglas said, placing
a cloth covered pail on the table. "We brought you some-

thing for your supper, but we won't be staying long. The days are getting shorter and shorter."

"Oh, please don't talk of leaving already. I'm glad you came. Would you like tea? Let me just finish and I'll build a fire and put the kettle on—"

"Please don't trouble yourself," Johanna, exquisite in a tailored, blue afternoon dress with a matching cape, interrupted while peeling off her gloves. "Mother can sit here in the rocking chair, and I'll take the stool, and you just relax. We didn't come to create more work. We just wanted to welcome you properly to Marietta, and apologize for not coming sooner."

McKenna sat down on her bed, truly surprised, but also wary because it had been years since she'd seen them. She wasn't sure if they harbored ill will towards her, either. "No apology needed. I didn't even know you were here until last weekend when I attended the party at Mrs. Bramble's." She drew a quick breath. "Which reminds me, thank you so much for the lovely bread and cake you sent with Sinclair on Sunday. That was much appreciated."

McKenna caught Johanna and Mrs. Douglas' swift exchange of glances but didn't know what that meant.

Silence stretched.

She drew another breath and tried to keep her tone bright. "It really is lovely to see you both. It's almost like being home."

"How are you faring so far our of town, my dear?" Mrs.

Douglas asked.

"Good," McKenna said, choosing to ignore Johanna's arched brow. "Of course, it's different from what I knew before coming here and, as you can imagine, I'm learning a great deal. I spend a lot of my free time writing letters. My friends in New York think I should write a book, *The Vassar Girl in Paradise Valley.*" Her laughter faded as she realized they weren't smiling with her.

She struggled to think of something to fill the uncomfortable quiet. "How is your business, Johanna? Your brother mentioned you have your own shop."

"She's doing very well," Mrs. Douglas answered. "Johanna can barely keep up with the orders."

"That's wonderful," McKenna said warmly.

"Yes, it is, but how are *you* getting on?" Mrs. Douglas glanced towards the hearth with the cast iron tripod. "I see you've been trying to cook over your fire. I did that many years ago."

"It's a challenge," McKenna admitted. "But, fortunately, I'm just cooking for me, and I'm learning as I go."

"If you have questions, I'm happy to help if I can, but I'll be honest, I'll never give up my stove. It's my favorite thing in the house. I can cook on it, and bake and I love how quickly I can make a cup of tea now."

"I certainly will never take a cup of tea for granted again," McKenna said firmly. "But do tell me about Marietta. I've only been to town a couple times. Are you happy there? Do you ever miss Butte?"

"It's not Butte," Johanna said, "but no place is."

"True," Mrs. Douglas added. "Yet we like Marietta. It's not a fancy place, but our circumstances are so much improved from Dublin Gulch. I'd never go back there."

"Your Butte was very different from others." Johanna unhooked her dark blue cape, revealing the elegant navy ruffle at the throat of her dress. "We don't live with the mining community. We are in town, and every day it seems as if there is something happening. The train changed everything and they've just put in street lights on Main Street. Soon all the houses on Bramble will have electricity, too."

"Oh, that's lovely. I'm envious." McKenna said, and it was true. She did not love her lanterns. It made reading and needlework harder, tiring her eyes. "Sinclair mentioned your dress shop. He said your business is quite successful."

"It's growing, and its almost always word of mouth. I have all the latest magazines and so if someone needs a new dress, or a wedding gown, they come to me. I will order fabric for them, too. I enjoy my work very much." Johanna glanced around the small cabin. "And you? Do you enjoy your work?"

McKenna nodded. "I like teaching, yes."

"You spent enough time in school," Johanna said, nose wrinkling. "But it seems disappointing that even with all your education you ended up here. This is so very... rustic."

McKenna heard the criticism but let it go, determined to keep things light. "When I'm not sure I'm happy here I pretend I traveled a great distance in a Conestoga wagon and have arrived after many months in the wilderness and thank God for my snug cabin with its lovely stone hearth." She smiled. "Sometimes it helps, sometimes it doesn't."

Johanna wasn't smiling. "You're not afraid living alone out here? You don't have any neighbors close by."

"I have a good deadbolt on my door."

Mrs. Douglas frowned. "My dear, but where is all your firewood? Where are your provisions? We've had good weather but it won't be long before the first hard storm hits, and I worry you're not prepared."

"I'm low on firewood now but, in general, the boys at school have been very good at keeping my woodpile stocked, and one my students' families, they have dairy cows, and we've worked out an agreement where I write letters for them and help keep their books and in return once a week they bring me fresh milk and eggs and cheese—and every two weeks a bit of butter. It's very good butter, too."

"And bread? Do you make it yourself?" Mrs. Douglas asked.

"I've tried." McKenna grimaced. "It's nothing like yours, so I mostly make biscuits or cornbread, but it works when I'm hungry."

"Oh, McKenna," Johanna sighed. "If only you'd been more careful in New York! I'm so sorry to see you like this."

McKenna's cheeks went hot. She couldn't bear the pity. "I should have, yes. You're absolutely right. But, I'm surprisingly content in my cabin, teaching at the school. On weekends I walk to the store in Emigrant and mail my letters and chat with Mr. Bottler's clerk and I'm happy. Maybe I'll feel differently when I'm snowed in, but right now I feel blessed."

"*Blessed?*"

She nodded. "Compared to many women I am in a most enviable position."

Johanna looked perplexed. "How can you possibly believe that?"

McKenna gestured to the door and beyond. "I'm independent. I have a job, a home. My superintendent, Mr. Egan, said he's quite pleased with my work. My students respect me. Their parents are grateful I am here. All in all, I would consider myself most fortunate."

"But you don't know how to do this!" Johanna's voice sharpened. "You're not at all equipped to live out here, in a rustic cabin, on your own."

"Emigrant is five miles south. Marietta is ten miles north. I'm healthy and strong. Yes, I work hard, but my families keep an eye on me. And I have you, too, as friends, to offer me encouragement and support." McKenna smoothed her skirt, flattening wrinkles from her dress, a light green that had turned to gray with repeated washings. "Are you truly concerned for me, or are you unhappy that I am here?"

Johanna leaned forward. "Wouldn't you be happier in a city? Wouldn't being somewhere with music and theatres and lots of social activities be preferable to... this?"

"I wasn't offered a teaching position in a city. I was offered a position here." McKenna's gaze locked with Johanna's. "And, forgive me, but I'm confused. Are you worried about my safety, or is there something else troubling you? Because I was here for two months before you came to call on me, which makes me think that perhaps we are not on such... friendly... terms anymore."

"Surely, you're not surprised." Johanna's lips curved, but the smile didn't reach her eyes. "We were friendly because of my brother. *He* brought us together. I was there for you because he asked me to look after you."

"We were friends before Sinclair."

"But we wouldn't have been as close if it were not for him." Johanna seemed to struggle with the next words. "I just don't understand. You had everything. *Everything.* And you threw it all away."

"Would I like electricity and plumbing? Yes. But losing them isn't the end of the world—"

"And Sinclair?" Johanna interrupted. "What about him?"

It was like a slap across her face. McKenna jerked backwards, stung. For a moment there was just silence, the silence heavy and suffocating.

Mrs. Douglas murmured something to Johanna. But Johanna's chin jutted up, her expression hard.

"She had everything." Johanna repeated, looking from her mother to McKenna. "Including Sinclair. And she threw him away, along with the rest of it."

McKenna couldn't defend herself. Johanna was right. McKenna had been spoiled and selfish and utterly self-absorbed, so willful and preoccupied that she never stopped to think how her actions would impact others.

She hadn't just wounded Sinclair, she'd alienated his family, too. "I apologized to your brother when he drove me home last week, and I would like to apologize to you both as well. I am sorry, Mrs. Douglas, and I am sorry, Johanna, deeply sorry—"

"You don't owe us an apology," Mrs. Douglas interrupted. "Whatever was between you and my son is your affair, not ours. I do not wish to get in the middle, especially as he is doing quite well. I am just grateful he is out of the mines, and healthy, and happy. That is all I could wish for him. More health, and more happiness."

"What my mother isn't saying is that he is interested in someone," Johanna said bluntly. "She is a good match for him, too. Mother and I are quite fond of her and we believe she will make my brother happy."

McKenna exhaled, stunned. For a moment, she couldn't breathe, or think. She sat frozen until little spots danced before her eyes.

Mrs. Douglas spoke to her daughter in a low voice, the

words unintelligible, but Johanna just shrugged her off. Mrs. Douglas looked away, expression pained.

McKenna shivered, suddenly chilled. She started to her feet to add a log to the fire when she remembered there was no fire, and frankly, now, when she had an audience, wasn't the time to try to build one. "He didn't mention her to me," she said at length.

Mrs. Douglas's voice dropped. "He is a private man."

McKenna felt so much in that moment—surprise, disappointment, confusion—she didn't know what to say. McKenna caught the way they exchanged glances.

She forced herself to speak. "So he is courting?"

Another glance between mother and daughter.

"We shouldn't say too much." Johanna ducked her head. "I don't want to distress you."

"Sinclair would never shame you," Mrs. Douglas added. "He will always be protective of you."

Johanna's lips compressed. "Maybe too protective, because it's important that he thinks of her now. I'm not saying this to hurt you, or punish you, but if his relationship is to progress, he must think of her. Not you."

"Of course," McKenna murmured, her pulse thumping hard. She could feel the intense drumming everywhere—in her veins, her heart, her head. "The relationship... it's become quite serious?"

"They are not yet engaged, but it's our hope it will happen soon. Maybe over the holidays," Mrs. Douglas said.

Johanna nodded. "There is no reason for him to wait. He's financially stable. He has an excellent piece of land. He's doing well with his cattle. There is nothing to prevent him from marrying and having children." She gave McKenna a long look. "Nothing should come between him and his happiness."

McKenna's lips parted, closed. It was none of her business. She had no right to ask. They owed her no explanation, either.

But McKenna couldn't remain silent. "Is she from here? Or from Butte?"

Mrs. Douglas looked at her daughter. Johanna shrugged.

Mrs. Douglas hesitantly asked, "Are you sure you want to know this, my dear? We don't want to upset you."

McKenna seriously doubted that. Her voice firmed. "I'd rather hear it from you than a stranger."

"I would be the same." Johanna lifted her gloves and began to pull one back on. "Mr. Burnett, Ellie's father, is from Texas. He came north with one of the big cattle drives and then stayed, buying land around Emigrant. He sent for his family. They had some trouble after arriving, and Mrs. Burnett died, leaving Miss Burnett to manage her father's household."

McKenna could hear the admiration in Johanna's voice. "You like her."

"She's a good match for Sin." At first Johanna sounded apologetic, but then she added, more defiantly. "She respects him."

"They're equals in every way," Mrs. Douglas added.

McKenna suddenly knew what they were saying. This wasn't a friendly social call. They'd come to make sure she understood how things were in Marietta. They were letting her know this wasn't her town, and were warning her away. She was to keep her distance from Sinclair.

AFTER JOHANNA AND Mrs. Douglas left, McKenna sat on her front porch and watched the sun drop, the long gold rays gilding the jagged peaks of the Absaroka range. She wouldn't let herself think about Johanna and Mrs. Douglas' visit. She wouldn't let their words hurt. No, she'd enjoy the beautiful valley and appreciate everything God had given her.

A sense of humor. A love for adventure. A job. Friends.

She was going to be just fine.

She breathed in the crisp, autumn air. Winter was coming. And the fireplace wasn't going to clean itself, either.

Suppressing a sigh, McKenna headed back into the cabin and finished cleaning the fireplace. She then carried in fresh wood, stacking the logs against the stone hearth, before heading back out to get more wood. She kept working, making each armful bigger and heavier than the last until she couldn't carry one more load, and then she sat down on her stool and pressed her knuckles to her mouth finally able to admit that the visit this afternoon from Sinclair's family had hurt.

And Johanna could say what she wanted, but they *had* been friends, hadn't they?

McKenna thought back, remembering studying together, and sitting side by side during choir. She'd had Johanna over to her house on numerous occasions, and yes, they'd talk about Sinclair, but that was because Johanna would mention him, sharing something funny, and just possibly outrageous, mentioning his work periodically, but never revealing anything negative, conscious that McKenna's father owned the mine. Those brief mentions would tease and yet sustain McKenna for another week, with weeks turning into years. Of course there were the rare occasions when McKenna would glimpse Sinclair at a school concert or picnic. He couldn't attend most due to work, but every now and then he'd appear at a school social, and her heart would beat faster, and she'd try to watch him without anyone knowing she watched him.

On those rare occasions, McKenna and Sinclair always managed to exchange a word or two. It was never anything serious or substantial, either, but just being near Sinclair filled McKenna with warmth and an almost unbearable longing. She didn't know what she wanted from Sinclair. She just knew she wanted something more. She knew he could give her more.

But Johanna? Were they ever truly friends, or had she befriended Johanna for selfish reasons?

Years ago, just before Johanna had left school to work, McKenna confessed to Johanna that she hadn't been a good enough friend.

Johanna made a face. "You mean, because you like my brother?"

McKenna had nodded, her face hot with embarrassment.

"I've always known you're interested in my brother, just as he's interested in you." Johanna's smile faded. "But we also know your father will never approve of Sinclair as a suitor—"

"We don't know that!"

"Oh, we do. I do. Why would he approve Sinclair as a husband, if he wouldn't even permit me to be your friend?"

McKenna didn't know what to say, because Johanna was right. Her father was happy to put the poor Irish immigrants to work, but he didn't want them in his home.

"I'm sorry," she whispered.

"Don't be sorry. Just don't hurt him."

But she had, hadn't she?

No wonder Johanna didn't want to pretend to be friends anymore. McKenna didn't blame her.

CHAPTER EIGHT

O N NOVEMBER EIGHTH, Montana became the forty-first state and part of the union. Montana's governor proclaimed the day a holiday and all banks and schools closed so that the public could celebrate.

McKenna was eager to join in the festivities planned in downtown Marietta, and happily accepted an invitation from the Hoffmans to ride in their large wagon. The Hoffmans had a big family, and four of their six children were McKenna's students. The boys teased her most of the way to town, saying that a New York lady shouldn't be so excited about Montana's statehood. She teased them back saying she'd been born in Montana and had more Montana in her little pinky then they did in their entire body.

Mr. Hoffman laughed, and Mrs. Hoffman asked about Butte, saying she'd heard it was such a beautiful city, and she hoped to go there one day. They were all in great spirits when they reached town. Red, blue, and white fabric arches ran the length of Main Street, with patriotic ribbons wrapped around the tree trunks and any available pole. Flags hung from the second story windows while red, white, and blue bunting decorated the windows of businesses on Main.

At the courthouse an enormous flag flew, the flag proudly bearing the forty-first star for the brand new state. The forty-first star was not an official count, and they'd all been warned it wouldn't be an official count as Washington was to become a state three days later, but the forty-first star meant something to everyone in Marietta that day.

It seemed that the entire community had gathered downtown for the coronation of Miss Copper Mountain, parade, and speeches. McKenna wanted to buy a bag of warm nuts from the man at the corner of the courthouse, but she didn't have five cents to spare and shook her head regretfully when he held the treat out to her.

In the distance a trumpet sounded, followed by the rat-a-tat-tat of a drum, and the crowd enthusiastically shifted from the park to Main Street, lining both sides of the road to enjoy the parade.

McKenna smiled and cheered with everyone else as the band marched down Main Street, followed by a buggy with dignitaries, and then a handsome gleaming carriage decorated with paper flowers and filled with the pretty girls who were princesses in Miss Copper Mountain pageant. Marietta was celebrating statehood in style, and McKenna could only imagine the celebration in Butte. The world was changing. Four new states were being added to the union from the Northwest Territory, and the possibilities were endless.

Suddenly aware that she was being watched, McKenna

turned her head, her gaze scanning the crowd. No one was looking at her, all eyes seemed to be on Marietta's fire department's horse and wagon decorated in red and blue ribbon. And then she saw them—Johanna and Mrs. Douglas and another young woman that looked to be a few years younger than McKenna and Johanna. They were standing just a few feet from her on the same side of the street, and as soon as Johanna saw she'd drawn McKenna's attention, she looked away without acknowledging her.

McKenna felt a pang, but then admonished herself. What did she expect after the visit on Saturday? That she and Johanna would be close friends? That was clearly not going to happen. She shouldn't be surprised that she'd been rebuffed.

But she was curious about the fashionably dressed young woman standing arm in arm with Johanna. The girl was tall and slender, with mounds of gleaming auburn hair, and dazzling, light-colored eyes. In her fitted green coat and stylish hat, she was far more beautiful than any of the young ladies in today's Miss Copper Mountain pageant.

Was this the Ellie that Sinclair was courting?

McKenna's heart fell at the thought, and yet she could see why Sinclair would be attracted to her. She was young and exceptionally pretty and she drew the attention of several men around her.

Suddenly McKenna didn't want to be standing on Main Street watching a small town parade. She was surrounded by people and yet she felt impossibly alone.

She slipped to the back and walked along the wall, escaping the crowd, having no destination in mind but just desperate to move.

It was a great deal of work pretending not to need people. It was exhausting trying to appear content with her life.

She wasn't content. She wasn't at all happy living alone. This wasn't the life she'd ever wanted but it was the life she had now and she was determined to make it work.

She would make it work, and trust that one day it would be different, and that she would have... more... again. A husband. Children. Family. Love.

Love.

Her eyes burned and she lifted her chin, blinking hard. She focused on the shining dome in the distance, the dome capping the handsome new courthouse that served Crawford County. She could just make out the patriotic swags of red, blue, and white bunting at each window of the second story windows.

"Hello, pretty little miss." A man who'd clearly enjoyed too much to drink at Grey's Saloon tipped his hat at McKenna and fell in step next to her.

She ignored him and kept walking, knowing conversation would just encourage him.

But the man needed no encouragement, not when he had whiskey on his breath. He walked closer, pressing almost against her. McKenna tried to walk faster but the parade had ended and the crowds were now shifting on the sidewalk making movement more difficult.

"You're not very friendly, are you?" The man slurred, his hand going to her elbow.

She shrugged him off and tried to step around two elderly woman but couldn't manage to get past before the drunkard reached for her again.

"Why are you acting like that? Why not be a bit friendlier on such a special day?"

McKenna turned her head, stared down the man. "Leave me be, sir."

"Wait, I know you." He grabbed her arm, holding her still. "Aren't you Frasier's girl? You're that one who—"

"I do not know you. Unhand me immediately!"

Suddenly Sinclair was there at her side. She hadn't seen him in the crowds, but his deep voice was unmistakable. "Let her go, Finch, before you permanently lose that arm."

Finch obeyed without hesitation. He stepped away, quickly, hands lifting. "Hey now, Mr. Douglas, no need remove that arm from my body. I'll never get any work done that way."

"It won't be much of a loss," Sinclair answered. "You don't get much work done with it."

"Now that's not fair, Mr. Douglas. You know I work hard—"

"When you're sober, and that's not often. Go home. Stop accosting ladies or I promise you, I'll be at your door and you won't like that." His voice roughened. "Nor will your wife."

Finch mumbled a garbled apology and turning around, fled.

McKenna's heart was still pounding as Sinclair focused on her. "He didn't hurt you, did he? Because if he did—"

"I'm fine," she answered, and she was.

Her pulse wasn't just racing out of fear. Yes, Mr. Finch had been a nuisance, but he hadn't frightened her as much as irritated her. Her heart was beating double fast because Sinclair was here, at her side. "And you were magnificent."

His blue eyes gleamed, creases fanning at the corner of his eyes. "You obviously do not get enough entertainment here."

"I don't," she admitted with a wry smile, "but you were impressive. And, tell me, if he'd manhandled me much more, would you have removed his arm?"

"Yes, absolutely. Just glad I didn't have to. He has five little Finches at home and I feel for them."

"He worked for you?"

"He did. I fired him for intoxication after repeated warnings."

"So he's unemployed now?"

"No, the new mine manager rehired him, at half of what he made before, but why not? Cheap labor."

"I hear your sarcasm."

His broad shoulders shifted. "You can't be weak when

you're managing a mine, and you're not there to be a friend. You're responsible for every life in that shaft and those tunnels. The men down below are dependent on management to ensure that machinery and equipment are in excellent condition and that safety protocols are being followed. You have to timber correctly, you have to muck correctly, you have to mine correctly. You hire a drunkard and he makes a mistake—and the men he's working with pay the price."

"Mr. Finch made a mistake," she said, understanding now where he was going.

"Yes."

"What happened?"

He shook his head, expression grim. "It's bad. It's tragic. You don't want to know."

"But I do. It's my father's company, and even if my father has disowned me, my last name still is Frasier."

"No one died that day, but one man lost a leg, and the other was blinded. Neither will ever work again."

"And my father? What does he do in those situations?"

"Nothing. He's not responsible."

"Did he provide anything for the families?"

Sinclair laughed shortly, no humor in the sound. "Come, sweetheart, you know your father better then that."

"What of the families?"

"You're the most intelligent woman I've ever known. Stop asking questions you know the answers to."

Heat rushed to her cheeks. She didn't know whether to feel flattered or not. "I'm sorry, and I apologize for my father—"

"They are all like that, McKenna. And not just the mine owners, but the industrialists across the country. There is no protection for the men that labor, and there is no help for the families that lose their husbands to due work injuries, or diseases like miner's consumption."

"That's what killed your dad, wasn't it?"

He shot her a sharp look. "Who told you that?"

"Johanna."

Sinclair shook his head, and exhaled. "The crowds are maddening. Shall we walk?" He held out his arm.

She took his elbow, relishing his warmth, and close proximity. She felt almost guilty for feeling so happy. He'd just told her terrible things and yet she was with him, walking with him, moving away from the crowds, west down Second Street. McKenna wasn't sure where they were going, not did she really care. It just felt so good to feel good.

"How did you get into town?" he asked, as they approached Front Street. They'd left the worst of the crowds behind. It was easy to walk now. No one was there to slow their progress or overhear their conversation.

"The Hoffmans brought me. Not sure if you know the family."

"They are one of my neighbors," he answered. "A nice family."

"They are," she agreed, "and they are one of the families that look after me. Mrs. Hoffman is always sending a bit of butter or cheese with the boys to school. I'm grateful for—" She broke off as Sinclair's arm flexed, muscle bunching beneath her hand as he stopped abruptly and lifted her from the street and onto the wooden sidewalk just as a horse and buggy turned the corner sharply, nearly running them down.

Sinclair muttered something about women drivers and McKenna clucked disapprovingly. "Just because she was a woman it doesn't mean women can't be excellent drivers."

"Can be, yes."

"Men aren't always better."

"When it comes to driving—"

"No. It's not a skill connected to one's gender."

"A certain degree of strength is required."

"Not as much as you'd like to think. Maybe if you have a runaway horse, then yes. But otherwise, its skill and control, and women can be masterful drivers."

His lips curved as he smiled down at her. "Are you one of those feminists, Miss Frasier?"

She smiled up at him. "Would it shock you to know I was, Mr. Douglas?"

His laugh was soft and low and sent a delicious shiver through her. "No. I fully expect you to be marching one day for the vindication of women's rights."

If she hadn't already loved him, she would have then. "You don't sound horrified."

"I suppose I would, if it was Johanna. But you… that's always been you."

"So I can have rights, but Johanna shouldn't?"

"I didn't say that." He was moving again, and they stepped off the curb and crossed the street. "I just don't see it being a cause that Johanna would fight for right now. But you, you've always looked for a cause."

"Have I?" she asked, glancing up into his face. He was so handsome it made her heart hurt a little bit.

"Wasn't I your very first cause?"

"You were never a cause, Sin."

"I'm not so sure about that."

They were next to the train depot with the railroad tracks behind. Sinclair paused and asked, "Are the Hoffmans taking you home?"

"Yes. I'm to the meet them in front of the courthouse at half past four."

"It's not yet three now." He glanced across the street, frowned, and then looked back at her. "Have you had anything to eat?"

"I'm waiting until I get home."

"Which means you do not have money to eat."

"That's not what it means. It means I had a substantial breakfast and I'm able to wait until evening for my dinner."

"So soup, roast, vegetables and what not, are unappealing?"

Her mouth watered. Her stomach had been growling for

hours. "I could probably eat a light bite."

"Soup and roast and vegetables?"

"And cake, if they had it."

He grinned. "McKenna, you haven't changed. Come. Let's see if The Graff can seat us."

As Sinclair escorted McKenna over the railroad track on the way to the Graff Hotel, Marietta's grandest hotel, the wind picked up, tugging at McKenna's bonnet, and pulling at the dark coat that covered her simple tweed walking dress. She laughed as her bonnet flew back, and laughed again as her coat flapped open over her skirts.

"A storm is moving in," he said, seeing the clouds gathering over the Absarokas. "I don't mind as long as the rain holds off until we get home."

A paper wrapper scuttled past, and then they were climbing the steps to the hotel's entrance. He'd been to the Graff numerous times for a meal or a drink in the bar, McKenna was the first woman he'd ever brought here. It somehow seemed appropriate that she be the first as there was no place finer in Crawford or Park County. German businessman Albert Graff had purchased the land five years ago and almost immediately broke ground, but the catastrophic winter storms of 1885 slowed progress, as the heavy, wet snow accumulated too quickly on the roof, bringing the roof down, and destroying the handsome lobby and elegant ballroom.

But Albert had the hotel repaired, finished, and open in time for the summer tourists three years ago, and it continued to be a popular draw for tourists craving a bit of luxury after a visit to Yellowstone.

The hotel management knew Sinclair, but then nearly everyone in Marietta knew him, and he was immediately given a table in the handsome bar as the main restaurant was closed for the holiday.

Sinclair had noticed that people watched their progress across the hotel lobby, and now they were drawing attention in the bar. He wasn't surprised, though. Even in her severe brown coat and sturdy tweed walking dress, McKenna glowed. Maybe it was because the dark colors contrasted with her pale ivory skin, or maybe it was because whenever she looked up at him, her eyes sparkled. Or maybe it was because she was simply breathtakingly beautiful.

"Am I imagining it, or are people staring?" she whispered, as he helped her coat.

"They were aware of you at the Brambles, too."

"Yes, but that was disapproval. Do all these people disapprove of me, too?"

"Some might." He held her chair for her, and assisted the chair forward once she was seated. "Others just might find you dazzling."

She laughed. "Dazzling? Have you looked at me lately? I'm a proper spinster now."

"A spinster?"

"Yes. I'm twenty-five, and still single, and since I can't marry and teach, it seems I'm destined to remain a spinster."

"You could marry."

"I'd have to give up teaching, then, and I need income."

"You don't need income if you marry."

"I'm not sure I'd trust him to provide."

He lifted a brow but couldn't reply as the waiter had arrived at their table. Sinclair wanted to get back to the conversation so he instructed the waiter to bring them whatever they were serving for lunch, adding that he'd like a cider as well.

Sinclair glanced at McKenna. "Would you care for a cider or something sweeter? Sherry, maybe?"

She gave her head a slight shake. "Tea, please," she answered. "I'm still a little chilled from that wind."

She didn't look chilled, he thought, as the waiter moved on. Her cheeks were pink and her eyes were bright and she looked impossibly alive.

"What did you mean that you wouldn't trust your husband to provide?" he asked.

She shrugged and began taking off her gloves. "Not all husbands are good providers, and not all husbands are generous with their wives, making it difficult for women to manage the households properly. Most of my friends from school have married good men, but there are two who should have done better. One husband can't keep a job—"

"Why?"

"I'm afraid he's like your Mr. Finch."

"I see. And the other?"

"He's…" Her voice faded and her expression darkened.

"Yes?"

"Not who he pretended to be. He's not a kind man. He's quite mean-spirited and all think Frances should leave him, but she won't."

"Has she spoken to her father?"

"It seems her father was the same way."

"And what way is that?"

She didn't immediately answer. "Do you know it was only twenty years ago that men could legally beat their wives in every state?"

"Frances' husband beats her?"

"I'm getting sad. Let's not be sad on such a special day. Let's speak of something else." She managed a smile, but he thought it looked strained. "What did you think of the parade and speeches? Wasn't it exciting? And did you see those lovely girls in the pageant?"

"I missed the pageant and the speeches and only saw the tail end of the parade. I'd only just arrived when I spotted you."

"And Finch," she said her smile somewhat crooked.

If they weren't in a public place he would have reached out and touched her cheek, right where the small dimple flashed and then faded.

"And Finch," he murmured, wanting her safe, and settled, and happy.

There were good men to be found, too. He'd find her one, someone who'd take her west, someone who'd give her all the comforts she was accustomed to.

"Well, the celebrations were splendid," she said firmly. "I was impressed."

He'd forgotten how quickly emotion crossed her features, and how easily she smiled when pleased. There was nothing subtle about her. Maybe that was what made people react to her, both good and bad. "How would it have been in Butte?"

"I was thinking of Butte, earlier. Everything they do is grand there, so I imagine they would have had a larger parade, and a lot of musicians, bands from Dublin Gulch, and the Germans and the Scots."

"And more speeches."

"A great deal more speeches," she agreed.

The waiter returned with a tray of drinks and placed the tall glass of amber colored liquid in front of Sinclair, and the small china pot and teacup before McKenna.

Sinclair reached for his glass. "Do you mind me drinking?"

"Why would I?"

"You're not a member of the temperance movement? Most suffragists seem to be both."

"I wasn't as much of a progressive as I probably should

have been."

"No writing of pamphlets? No marching in streets?" he teased.

"I don't know anyone who did that, at least not in New York. Maybe Boston. Perhaps Philadelphia." Her lips curved. "Instead I was being fitting for costumes for fancy dress balls, both home and abroad."

He heard the mocking note in her voice. "You make it sound like a bad thing."

"Wasn't it? You were here, toiling in my father's mine, while I was going to parties and plays, with my only worry being what to wear next."

"I knew this was what you were doing."

"It didn't make you angry?"

"I was happy for you."

"Why?"

"I wanted you to have the world. And you did."

Her eyes suddenly glistened and she looked away, teeth sinking into her lower lip. "Don't say it like that," she whispered.

"What's wrong?"

She looked down, her thick black lashes hiding her eyes, the crescent shaped lashes brushing her cheek. "I hate how selfish I was—"

"I suspect your father will one day forgive you, particularly if you make an advantageous marriage."

"You seem quite determined to marry me off," she said

lightly. "And yet I see no suitors lining up outside my door."

"They would, if they thought you'd consider marrying one of them."

"Even with the stigma attached to my name?"

"California and Nevada are full of self-made men. And what do new millionaires want? They want a beautiful wife, to give them beautiful children."

"How nice for them."

"Not all men are vile, alcohol-soaked wife beaters."

"I'm sure not all are, but you forget something important. You forget me. I am not a woman that would make a good wife. I'm not docile and obedient. I've too many opinions and, Sinclair, I can keep my house tidy, but I don't love the domestic arts."

"You'd rather struggle on your own then be provided for?"

"If it means I can think my own thoughts and be my own person, yes."

"Don't you want to have a husband... a family?"

Her head jerked up and her gaze met his and held for the longest time. "No," she said at length. "I'm afraid I'm too selfish."

"Too selfish to love someone else?"

"Too selfish to give up my dream of how life is supposed to be."

"How is life supposed to be?"

She shook her head, shadows darkening her eyes.

His brow creased. He didn't understand, and he wanted to understand, but before he could pose another question, he spotted three familiar faces in the door. He'd seen them earlier, and he'd tried to draw McKenna away but somehow he and McKenna had been found. He knew who'd tracked them down. Johanna was determined to see Sinclair married to Miss Burnett, and soon.

"It looks like we will have company for lunch,' he said casually, before rising to greet his mother, Johanna, and Miss Ellie Burnett.

CHAPTER NINE

THE WAITERS QUICKLY drew a table over to create sufficient space for the additional ladies, and the three women, protesting that they never meant to sit down, sat down, skirts rustling, voices a murmur of feminine sound. Miss Burnett, McKenna discovered, was just as pretty up close.

McKenna fixed a smile on her face for the introductions, praying it was warm and cordial, even as she felt the cool undercurrents despite the civil greetings. It didn't help that she felt dreadfully guilty, as though she'd been caught doing something illicit.

And she had, if she were honest. He was single. She was single. He wasn't courting her, which created all sorts of problems for those preoccupied with deportment.

"It's begun to rain," Mrs. Douglas said. "It's a freezing rain, though. I think we'll see snow later."

The waiter went to order more pots of tea and soup and whatever else could be brought quickly as the storm was just going to get worse and Mrs. Douglas didn't think Sinclair would want to be out late.

"I'm not worried about the weather," he answered. "I'll be fine."

"What about you, my dear," Mrs. Douglas asked McKenna. "How are you getting home?"

"I'm to meet my family at the courthouse in half an hour," McKenna said, "but I wouldn't be surprised if they want to leave earlier, on account of the weather."

"You have family here?" Ellie interjected, surprised. "I had no idea."

"Oh, no. I was speaking of the Hoffmans. I teach four of their children. They are a ranching family in the valley, not far from Emigrant."

"I know the Hoffmans," Ellie answered. "My father's property isn't far from theirs. They have a dozen boys, I believe. Or something along those lines."

"I think there are six and, yes, all boys. I have the four older ones in my classroom, with two toddlers still at home."

Ellie turned to Sinclair. "Remember the Hoffmans summer picnic? Everyone had such a good time, no one wanted to leave, and then Mr. Deltman's boy pulled out a fiddle and everyone danced half the night." She smiled at him. "At least we did."

"I think that was the first time I've danced in years," he said. "Three dances and I was worn out."

"It wasn't three! We danced for hours."

He smiled, amused. "*You* danced for hours. You were quite popular, as ever."

McKenna's stomach rose and fell and she suddenly wanted to be anywhere but here, where lovely Ellie was making Sinclair laugh, and his family was hanging on every word, delighted by the repartee.

It would be rude to leave before her meal arrived, but she'd lost her appetite. Glancing out the small window, she could see the rain was turning to sleet and was coming down harder, and thicker. "The weather's turning foul," she said. "I don't think I should keep the Hoffmans waiting."

"You haven't eaten yet," Mrs. Douglas said. "Should I have them pack you something to take with you? Some bread and cold meats? Or maybe one of their meat pies? I'm sure the chef has something you could carry out."

"I'm not hungry. The tea was all I needed." McKenna rose, smiled at everyone, careful not to look at Sinclair, not wanting him to make eye contact. "It was so nice to see everyone, and a pleasure to meet you, Miss Burnett."

And then she hurried towards the door, collecting her coat on the way. She walked fast, blinking, so conflicted about leaving. She hated saying goodbye to Sinclair that way, and yet she couldn't just sit there and smile as if everything was fine. Things weren't fine. And Sinclair wasn't hers and she wasn't a good enough actress to act indifferent when Ellie Burnett flirted with him.

Footsteps rang behind her. Sinclair caught up with her half way across the marble and mahogany paneled lobby with the glittering chandeliers. "Let me at least help you with your coat," he said.

She refused to slow down. She flashed a taut smile in his direction. "I'm fine. I don't need help."

"You're practically running. Stop it." He caught her elbow, turned her to face him. His narrowed gaze swept her hot face. "You are upset. You're about to cry. What is the matter?"

"I'm not about to cry. I don't cry—"

"You not cry? Since when? You've always been emotional."

"Well, I don't cry anymore. Tears are useless. They change nothing."

He took her coat from her. "You were happy earlier."

"I was," she said. "Yes."

"What was said to upset you so much? Did my mother say something that I missed? Or was it Johanna? Tell me and I'll have a word with them."

"It was no one, Sinclair. There was nothing. It's been a long day and I work tomorrow and I am sure the Hoffmans will be waiting for me. It's better to go back early." Her voice cracked and she shook her head. "See? I'm just tired. Forgive me."

"*McKenna.*" He growled, voice pitched low.

Aware that others were watching, and that a couple just entering the hotel had slowed to listen, McKenna gave him a radiant smile. "Happy Statehood Day, Mr. Douglas. What a great day it's been for all."

THE SLEET TURNED the road to a muddy, slushy mess. It was slow going south, the wheels sticking in ruts, making the horses unhappy.

The Hoffman children who had been so lively on the way into town were morose and miserable on the way home, shivering and complaining until their father threatened to take a switch to them if they made another sound.

It was dark by the time they reached the plot of land with her house and the school. McKenna thanked the Hoffmans for their kindness as she climbed down from the wagon, and bundling her coat tighter, she dashed across the crunchy ice coated grass for her front porch.

Opening her door she was immediately struck by the warmth, and then the glow in the corner, opposite the big hearth.

She had a stove.

She had a *stove*.

McKenna closed the door and crossed to the new stove, gleaming in the corner. A tall, black chimney ran straight up to the ceiling, carrying the smoke above the roof.

She walked towards the stove, pulling off her bonnet and then her gloves, thinking she'd never seen anything half so beautiful. It definitely wasn't the biggest model as there were huge cook stoves available, or the fanciest heating stove, but this narrow stove was perfect for her needs as it took up very little floor space and still had a lovely flat plate for cooking and heating water. She noticed the bin next to the stove already filled with chopped wood so she could keep the fire burning tonight.

Her eyes filled with tears as the heat penetrated her coat, and she sank in front of her stove, hands outstretched, letting the warmth surround her. It was without doubt the most lovely gift she'd ever been given.

She knew who'd done this, too. It was why he wasn't in town today for the festivities, only arriving at the end of the parade. It must have taken him most of the day to lug the stove into the cabin and cut the hole in the roof and mud around the chimney to ensure it was secure and the cabin properly ventilated.

He'd missed the celebrations for her, to do something for her.

It made her throat squeeze closed and her chest feel tender. He'd never said a word, either.

She'd been given many lovely gifts in her life but nothing had ever meant so much. And not just because it was the very thing she needed most, but because it was given by the one person who'd once understood her best.

Who might still understand her best.

He was her friend. He'd always been her friend. She'd never appreciated him, though. She'd taken him for granted.

He was right, what he'd said coming home from the Brambles. He deserved better. And he did. He deserved a woman who would put him first.

Beautiful auburn-haired Ellie Burnett came to mind.

McKenna's eyes stung and she closed her eyes, chasing the image of Ellie away.

McKenna was jealous. Not that she had the right to be jealous, but Sinclair was hers. He'd always been hers.

Why hadn't she married him when she'd had the chance?

MONDAY AFTERNOON MCKENNA remained at her desk after class had ended, taking advantage of the large workspace and excellent natural light to grade papers and plan her lessons for the rest of the month.

She'd just finished preparing the math lessons for the coming week when the door to her classroom opened and McKenna lifted her head, certain it was one of her forgetful students back to retrieve missing lunch pail or book, but it wasn't a student. It was Sin.

He was so big as he filled the doorway. Tall, broad shouldered, with the thick blond hair and masculine jaw.

Her pulse jumped and she held her breath, taking him in, feeling his full impact.

For a moment, she just felt the fierce hammer of her heart, her blood drumming in her veins, making her head light, and her emotions hot. She couldn't help her response, either. It was as much as part of her, as it was a part of them.

Whether she was a girl watching him on the football field, or sitting with him in desks too small, listening to him read from a baby primer, she'd been dazzled by him, responding to him as if he were the moon and stars.

It was such a strong reaction, so intense, that it shook her to the core.

The attraction was overwhelming, and it had overwhelmed her even more when she was a young girl. How did one live feeling so much? How did one survive life when it made them feel so tender all the time?

"Hello," she said, finding her voice as she put her pen down. "I don't suppose you've come about a missing lunch pail. I have three at the back."

He smiled crookedly, white teeth flashing. "None of those are mine, Miss Frasier."

"I see. I will have to work harder at finding their homes."

He walked towards her, unbuttoning his heavy coat, revealing the blue work shirt beneath. The blue was almost the same color as his eyes.

She loved his eyes. She loved his face. Such a beautiful face. Such a beautiful man. "By the way, I owe you thanks. You shouldn't have—"

He sat down on the corner of a desk in the front row directly across from her. "I don't know what you're talking about."

"My new stove?"

He shook his head. "Not me."

She stared at him, searching his solemn expression, and just when she was beginning to doubt herself, he winked at her, and her heart gave another thump.

"Okay, don't claim the good deed," she said, "but I'm grateful. Very, very grateful. I don't think I've slept that well in weeks, and then each morning I have hot water in no time. It's a miracle."

"It hasn't smoked too much?"

"Not at all."

"Good."

He extended a leg. "What happened at the Graff during lunch to make you leave so quickly?"

She moved her ink well back. "I was worried that I'd miss the Hoffmans."

"You didn't leave because of the Hoffmans. You left because my mother and sister arrived."

"Remember how it was getting stormy? There was rain and sleet and snow forecasted—"

"I know you waited over an hour at the courthouse park for the Hoffmans. Mrs. Bramble saw you and was worried you'd been forgotten."

"They ran late."

"And you ran out to be early."

"They were my ride, Sinclair."

"Come on. This is just going round and round. Tell me what happened at the Graff. I want to know why you left so abruptly. Everything was good, and then it wasn't once my mother and sister arrived, and I want to know what they said or did to make you leave so quickly."

"They did nothing, I promise."

"McKenna, you bolted like a rabbit."

She shrugged impatiently. "Fine. I wasn't comfortable once they joined us. I thought it best to go before things became more awkward."

"You were once friends with Johanna."

"Not anymore."

"Why not?"

"They came to see me, you know. A week after the Brambles' party."

"My mother mentioned it to me. She said you'd been at work when they stopped by so they didn't stay long."

"Yes, I was cleaning the hearth. I was filthy." McKenna didn't know what else to say. She didn't want to create trouble. Her position felt precarious as it was.

"You weren't happy to see her?"

"I was quite happy to see her. I hugged them both, despite being black with soot, and I was very touched that they'd remembered me, and brought me freshly baked bread and preserves. It was such a treat."

"And?"

"Let's not continue this. It's not going to please you. At least, it doesn't please me. It's upsetting. I don't want controversy and yet every time I turn around, I am at the center of some conflict and I can't do it. I can't live like this with people constantly at me, talking about me, criticizing me at every turn—"

"What did my mother say?"

"I'm not good for you, Sinclair," she said bluntly.

"What does that even mean?"

"Your family remembers how I hurt you—"

"Pfft. I'm not a child."

"Yes, but they're women, and women have memories of elephants. We women never forget anything."

"So something was said to you that hurt you, because you are hurt. That's why you rushed away from lunch. Your feelings were hurt which is why you didn't want to eat with them."

"They are far easier to be with than Miss Burnett."

He glanced up at her. "What can you possibly have against Miss Burnett? She's well liked by everyone."

"I'm sure she is. She sounds very popular which is probably why she danced all night long."

The corners of his mouth curved. "You're jealous."

"I'm not jealous. She's your sister's good friend and your... you know. There's no reason to be jealous of your... whatever she is."

He kept smiling at her. "I had no idea you were the jealous sort."

"I am not jealous. How can I be jealous? I had my chance. You gave me a chance—"

"Did Johanna say I was spending time with Miss Burnett?"

"Aren't you?" she snapped.

He grinned and shook his head, and began wandering

around her classroom. He moved with easy grace, so very comfortable in his skin.

She watched him stop at her narrow bookcase with the row of books. He pulled out one dark green volume and leafed through it for a moment before putting it back.

"This brings me back to when we were in school." He looked over at her. "Remember when you taught me to read?"

"You already knew how to read."

"Not well."

"I just think you were bored by the children's stories. You needed something more interesting."

"So you had me read Horatio Algers."

"Should I not have?"

"It put ideas in my head. It made me think I could be one of those self-made men." He leaned against the wall. "I've often wondered if that was intentional. Were you trying to inspire me? Did you want me to want more?"

"I assumed you wanted more. Isn't that why your parents left Ireland? To have more than they could have there?"

"I'm not talking about my parents. I'm talking about you and me." His gaze met hers and held. "Of all the books you could have had me read, why the Alger rags-to-riches novels? Why not history books, or a Mark Twain novel?"

"Should I not have?"

"Those stories were a tease. An American fantasy. Most men will never have that kind of success. Most men will never have great wealth."

"You think I set you up for failure?"

"I haven't failed. I don't live on Millionaire Row, but I have five hundred acres and one hundred head of cattle and a comfortable home. I have no debt. I have no employer. I answer to no one."

"You have what your parents came to America for. Prosperity, freedom, security."

"You wanted this for me," he said.

Her gaze traveled slowly over his handsome face—the broad brow, strong cheekbones, square jaw—and she nodded once. "I did."

"You believed I could be more," he added.

Her eyes stung and her chest burned. A lump filled her throat. "With or without money, you are more." She exhaled painfully. "You've always been more."

Her gaze locked with his.

"But not enough to marry me," he added.

She touched the tip of her tongue to her upper lip, wetting it. Her mouth was so dry.

She didn't know how to explain everything that had happened when she still didn't fully understand. "It wasn't that simple."

"I want to know," he answered, crossing his arms over his chest. He was so big and ruggedly beautiful, filling her classroom with energy and vitality. Even from across the room she could feel that intensity all the way through her.

"I'm not a simpleton—"

"Never said you were! And I didn't go away to escape you," she said, and it was true.

Her desire to earn a college degree and travel and be someone had little to do with love. She had loved Sin. She couldn't remember a time she didn't love him. But she struggled then—as she did now—with the idea that love meant one couldn't want more, that love meant she was supposed to give up her own dreams. And so she'd reached for more, and failed. Gambled and lost. Not just Sin, but her family, and her position in society, leaving her with even less than what she'd started with.

"I went away confident in us, confident that we would have forever," she added.

"And then you realized there was a great deal more to life than Butte and copper mines."

"I love New York, and London, and Venice." She hesitated. "I'd be somewhere and wish you were there, and then I'd wonder if you'd even want to go to those places."

"Don't feel a need to go to any of them."

"I thought that would be your answer."

"And you wanted these places more than me?"

"No. But I began to worry that I hadn't been honest with you—"

"That's fairly obvious."

"And that maybe I wasn't really what you wanted."

He looked at her a long moment. "So help me understand—what did I want?"

"A wife. Someone to have your children and make you dinner and do your laundry and make sure you were comfortable."

Sinclair continued his walk around the schoolroom. "That is what wives do."

"It sounds so much like drudgery."

"The children, or the laundry, or the loving?"

"You know what I mean."

"No, to be honest, I'm not sure I do."

"Loving you—" She broke off, flushing.

She'd almost said that it was easy, that it was the most natural thing she knew how to do. But it wasn't entirely true.

Loving him was complicated. Wanting him was easy but crossing the divide was hard. He wanted the earth and she wanted the stars. He put down roots and she wanted to fly.

How to reconcile their differences?

How to love him and not lose herself?

How to be what he needed and not feel trapped?

Her silence seemed to frustrate him. He walked another few steps before planting his feet to read the day's lessons still up on the blackboard.

"You've had it so easy," he said finally. "You might as well be royalty. I don't think you ever had to prepare a meal for yourself, or do your own laundry until you arrived here."

She winced at his tone, but he spoke the truth. "Yes. You're right."

He touched the date on the blackboard, smudging the chalk. "I think I'm beginning to understand what happened when you went to New York. You left Vassar and realized you had choices. You didn't have to choose me. You didn't have to choose poverty—"

"No."

"Let me finish." He faced her. "You saw your friends marry wealthy men, and you have opportunities most women would never have, and you realized that even though you loved me, you didn't love me enough to be like my mam."

She swallowed hard. Again, he saw far more than she'd imagined.

After her mother died and she returned to New York, the fantasy began to wear thin. Her mother's death had been slow and agonizing, and the wasting away of a woman's life had terrified her.

It was hard enough losing her mother in their elegant, modern home. Imagine dying in a place without the conveniences of running water and electricity? Imagine trying to nurse someone without being able to afford help, never mind excellent doctors?

And then there was love. The intense desire, the dizzying attraction. She wanted him, and craved his mouth on hers, and his arms around her, holding her close.

But would desire survive illness, poverty, and the dangers of childbirth?

And what if he died in the mines? What if he died like his father had, how would she raise their children? How well would she make ends meet? "You are content with so much less."

"I'm content with less because I've never had more. It's not that I enjoy less. It's that more isn't easily attained."

She glanced down and saw she'd accidentally knocked her pen from the inkwell, splattering black ink across her lesson plan book. She dabbed the wet ink dry. "It's all true. Everything you've said. I didn't want to be poor. I didn't know how to marry and keep a house and not have help. I was scared to give birth to baby after baby—"

"You should have just told me. All you had to do was write me. Tell me you'd changed your mind, and that you didn't love me—"

"But I did love you."

"All the more reason for you to have written that letter, and let me know how things were, and not to wait for you any longer."

She closed her eyes and nodded, because he was right. Absolutely right. She'd owed him that much, and more.

"I should have been honest," she said, opening her eyes, only to discover she was speaking to an empty room. Sinclair was gone and his departure was so abrupt it felt as if he'd taken a sledgehammer to her heart.

CHAPTER TEN

THE WEEK PASSED, and the weather had noticeably turned colder, the air sharper, the wind vigorous, constantly at play. Although Thanksgiving was still twelve days away, winter seemed impatient to arrive, with snow falling midweek.

The light flurries had melted within a couple of hours, but McKenna fully expected that to change any time now, but before it did, she needed supplies, and someone to come look at her stove as it had begun to smoke a little bit.

These were the times McKenna wished she knew more practical things. For example, was it normal after time to have a little bit of smoke from one's stove? And if there was a problem, was it something she should be able to fix herself? She'd tried to inspect the chimney but she had no idea what she was looking for and just ended up with a filthy hands and face.

Thursday and Friday she avoided using her stove, planning on going to Emigrant Saturday to see if she couldn't hire someone to come out and look at her for her. And that someone would *not* be Sinclair.

She appreciated the gift of the stove—it had been incredibly thoughtful and generous gesture on his part—but she hadn't forgotten their conversation Monday afternoon, and she'd slept poorly since, still bruised from his abrupt departure.

He of all people should know her. He should know she'd never meant to hurt him. He should know there was nothing cold or calculating in her.

If anything she was too emotional, too impulsive, and being impulsive had disastrous results. Just take a look at her life, and the mistakes she'd made. It was time she grew up and learned from the past. And she was trying. She really was. Because, clearly, she didn't know men, or understand them at all. Bernard had opened her eyes, and then her father's scathing denouncement had broken her heart.

This year had made McKenna doubt everything she knew about men, and life, and even herself. She found herself questioning everything constantly, including her feelings for Sinclair.

She wanted him. That was simple.

She loved him. That was a given.

But could he forgive her for the past? And were they better suited now, or was there still too much conflict and tension? Deep down, she feared there might always be conflict and tension. Deep down, she feared that she'd never be what he wanted or needed, and that made her hold back from reaching out to him.

Yet, when alone, he was all she thought of. And not even when she was alone, but even when she was teaching, she'd be in the middle of a lesson, and she'd find herself thinking of him, wondering when she'd see him again, wanting to see him again, and she'd have to shake herself, and focus her thoughts.

But then he'd creep back in.

And she'd long for him to suddenly open the door and be there.

It was a secret wish... a dream...

Was it too much a dream?

If only she knew. If only she had someone she could talk to, as she needed advice. This wasn't something she could talk to Sinclair about, either. She'd disappointed him once. She couldn't do that to him again.

Friday night after school, McKenna wrote her friend Amelia, her best friend from Vassar. McKenna wrote her almost weekly, but she kept her letters cheerful, not wanting to worry Amelia who had enough to deal with as a newly-wed.

Sitting before the fire, McKenna put her pen to paper, keeping her tone light, writing a long, chatty, humorous letter intended to make Amelia laugh, and then at the very end, McKenna added a post script, asking Amelia how she dealt with a husband on a daily basis? Were men as mystifying as they seemed? How did Amelia manage her Mr. Harris?

Saturday morning, McKenna did her usual weekend

chores, before changing to walk into Emigrant to mail her letter pick up a few items from Mr. Bottler's store.

Emigrant had been founded by three emigrants that had arrived in August 1864 on the Bozeman Trail. When they discovered miners were already in the valley, they traveled deeper into the gulch, finding gold high on the side of what they all knew as Emigrant Peak. But winter was harsh and there wasn't a great deal of gold. The minters struggled but Frank Bottler, a savvy entrepreneurial sort, bought land and fenced in pastures for cows and pigs, planting crops, and created a store for those who were struggling to eek out a living in the remote valley. When the train tracks were laid to carry tourists to Yellowstone, the train made a stop in Emigrant so tourists could stock up one last time before they reached the rugged national park.

McKenna relied on Mr. Bottler's store far more than her students' families. Most local homesteaders couldn't afford to be dependent on others, which was why they had their own livestock and crops. McKenna was not about to plant anything, and she was grateful for the store as it gave her somewhere to go on the weekends and if she was lucky, she'd find someone pleasant to visit with.

Today when she dropped her letter off with the clerk at Bottler's, the clerk asked her to wait a moment. "I have a letter for you today, Miss Frasier."

McKenna was delighted. It had been over a month since she'd received any letters, and she hoped it might be a letter from Mary. She missed her sister, and she'd give anything to have an update from home. But it wasn't Mary who'd written. It was dear Amelia.

Before leaving Bottler's, McKenna asked the clerk if he knew of anyone who did repairs, or looked at things like chimneys as her new stove was smoking, and she didn't know if there was someone in Emigrant who fixed that sort of thing. The clerk promised to speak to Mr. Bottler, assuring her that between the two of them they'd find someone, but in the meantime, to refrain from lighting her stove until someone could look at it.

McKenna agreed and after purchasing a small bag of flour and some salt and a cup of sugar, walked back towards her cabin, making a detour before her road to go sit on the bank of the river. The trees lining the Yellowstone were beginning to drop their leaves and the riverbank shimmered gold.

She sat down on her favorite rock, the copper and gold leaves clouding around her and drew the letter from her pocket, smiling at the elegant script of her friend's name on the return address.

Mrs. Henry Harris

Lucky Amelia who'd made an excellent marriage. Mr. Harris wasn't just a successful banker, but he absolutely adored his wife.

McKenna unfolded the letter and began to read.

Dearest McKenna,

Everything is well here and I've been waiting to share my good news until I was feeling better, and I'm feeling better, so brace yourself, darling, because... I'm expecting! Mr. Harris could not be happier. I was not myself for the past few months but that's changed and I'm overseeing the preparations for the nursery, looking forward to welcoming our little one in late February.

I can't even begin to tell you how much I have been enjoying your letters. They lifted my spirits so much when I had to take to my bed. McKenna, you inspire me with your wit and humor, taking your difficult situation and turning it into an adventure. You were always an excellent writer at school and you have captured the true spirit of the Northwest Frontier perfectly. I can't wait until you finally visit Yellowstone and tell me everything. I look forward to your next letter.

Amelia

PS I hope you won't mind that I shared your last few letters with Mr. Harris, and he agreed with me that you are an exceptional storyteller and wondered if maybe you've missed your calling? Could you possibly be the next Mark Twain or Jack London? Mr. Harris believes he could get your letters published. It wouldn't be a great deal of money but every little bit would help, wouldn't it, my dear? Do let me know if you give Mr. Harris permission to act on your behalf, and also, if you would want to use your name or perhaps a pseudonym?

McKenna lowered Amelia's letter. Amelia was going to be a mother! Such exciting news.

And how exciting, too, that Mr. Harris thought that someone else would enjoy reading about McKenna's adventures in Montana.

McKenna doubted that anyone would pay her for them, but just the idea of having her stories published made her feel buoyant and optimistic. She'd have to write Amelia back right away, to congratulate her on her news, as well as address Amelia's questions.

Stuffing the letter into her coat pocket she began the walk home. If she could find someone to print the letters, should McKenna use a pseudonym? Would it be better if she did, or would using her real name maybe help her redeem herself? Maybe society would eventually forgive her.

But, then again, maybe no one would want to read her letters if they knew they were by her…

McKenna was still deep in thought when she approached the schoolhouse and her cabin beyond. A thud echoed in the clearing, and she frowned. Who could possibly be here? She heard another thud and another.

Was someone in her cabin?

And then she saw movement on her roof, and the horse tethered to a tree, and she didn't believe it. She couldn't believe it. It was Sinclair. The one person she didn't want help from, and how was it that he'd already arrived? She'd only left town an hour ago.

She marched across the field, hands knotted, but before she could speak he rose, straightening to his full height. He dwarfed her roof, broad shoulders silhouetted against the sky. "You should have told me," he called down to her. "Why didn't you send word to me? Why go to Bottler?"

His curtness put her teeth on edge, and any conciliatory thing she might have said was gone. "It's my stove, and I will ask for help from whomever I want to help me."

"It's not your stove. I gave it to the school district, for future teachers, not you." He knelt down, hammered a nail into a shingle. "And nobody but me touches my stove."

"Well, your stove is in my house—"

"The school district's house."

Her face flushed. Her temper blazed. "You're deliberately picking my words apart. Did you come all this way to fight with me?"

He hammered another nail before looking at her. "No. I came all this way to fix *my* stove."

"You're infuriating, Sinclair Douglas."

"*I'm* infuriating? How do you think I felt hearing that Bottler was looking for someone to send to the school teacher's house to fix a stove *I* installed?"

"This has nothing to do with you!"

"Maybe that's the problem. Maybe it should." He rolled up his sleeves higher on his arms before giving her a nod, dismissing her.

Entering her house, McKenna paced the floor. She

didn't know what to do with herself while he worked. The noise was deafening. The hammering made her lantern rattle and the framed photo on the mantle danced forward and then back.

McKenna took the silver framed picture off the mantle and put it on her table, and glanced down at the photograph of her with her father and Mary on the deck of a great ship on their first trip abroad.

In the picture, Father stood in the middle, his arm around each of them, and they were all wearing hats and smiling for the camera. Well, Father didn't smile for the camera, but he stood with his big chest puffed out, and proud gleam in his eye.

McKenna's hair was loose—something Mother wouldn't have liked—but Mother was in Butte, recovering from influenza and she'd sent them all off so she could recuperate properly. McKenna had always been close to her father, but on that trip they became friends. Father would talk to her about his business and politics and ask her opinions and she felt so grown up. Mary, on the other hand, was ten, and spent most of the trip complaining, either seasick or home-sick. Mary never went overseas again and McKenna couldn't wait for the next adventure.

McKenna looked up from the photograph, realizing the pounding on the roof had stopped. She waited a moment and there was just silence.

Opening the door she stepped out. Sinclair was off the

roof and putting his tools away in his horse's saddlebag.

"All done?" she asked.

"Yes. All should be right now. But I'd like to fire up the stove and check just to be sure."

She stepped aside, inviting him. "Would you like tea? Or something to eat?"

He rolled his sleeves back down, covering his corded forearms. "Did you buy food while you were out?"

"Why?"

"Because you have nothing here. Your cupboard is empty—"

"You looked in my cupboards?"

"I came inside first to examine the stove."

"And my cabinets, too, from the sound of it!"

"I worry about you." He went to the stove and built a quick fire. He turned to face her once the flames latched onto the wood. "You've always been thin, but you're bordering sickly—"

"Sickly?"

"I'm not the only one to have noticed. Bottler's clerk noticed today. He mentioned it to Bottler as well. People are worrying. They know how harsh the winter can be. You need to eat more, and you need to eat better, or you won't be strong enough to survive the cold, or a bout of the influenza."

"You are so full of cheer."

"Better I be honest now then have to apologize to you

when you're on your deathbed."

"If this is your idea of sweet talk—"

"I'm not courting you, no need for sweet talk. And if you had some friends, I would hope they'd tell you the same. That you need to eat better food, and more of it, and not just that crackling bread or shortening bread or whatever it is I understand you live on."

"I've become quite good at baking." She nodded at the small bag of flour on the counter, next to the pinch of salt and cup of sugar.

"You need meat, and eggs, and milk, too. Vegetables. And more of everything."

"I can't afford meat, but the Hoffmans—"

"Yes, they send eggs and cheese and such on occasion." He picked up his coat and slid it back on. "But those occasional gifts aren't going to sustain you. You need more eggs and milk, cheese and butter, along with meat."

"I'm sure you know that if I could afford all of that, I would eat it."

"Maybe you need to stop relying on the generosity of others, and learned to provide for yourself. Learn to hunt, and you could have rabbit or squirrel stew—"

"Oh, no. No. That sounds positively horrendous."

"Rabbit stew is delicious."

"I don't know. And squirrel?" She grimaced, a hand going to her throat. "Never. And I'm not going to hunt. I can buy what I need at the butcher."

"There is no butcher in Emigrant."

"Then Marietta."

"This isn't Butte. You are not your mother, or your mother's housekeeper. You can't afford to send for meat, and the butcher isn't going to carve you pretty steaks. You'd be lucky to buy an oxtail now and then. So, I'm going to do what someone should have done months ago. I'm going to show you how to survive on what's around you. Get your coat—"

"No." She shook her head. "Besides, I think all the squirrels just went into hiding."

"We'll get something, and then you'll prepare it."

"*I'll* prepare it?"

"I'll show you how to skin it."

She felt dangerously light-headed. "No, thank you."

"You can't be such a princess."

"I'm not a princess. I'm extremely practical. Which means I know my limits. I'll learn Greek and Latin—useless languages for someone like me—but I'll do it because I can. Skin an animal? Never. I didn't even like dissecting frogs in biology."

"You could eat a frog."

"I will not." Even in Paris she hadn't eaten frog's legs. It didn't matter how much butter and wine they were simmered in. She looked through the window and glanced up to the sky. It had grown darker, the clouds gathering, hanging low, hiding the mountain peaks. "Is it going to rain?"

"I don't care. I'm not leaving until we have something you can roast for supper."

"Well, I do, and I will not be hunting with you, Sinclair. If you must go shoot things, go do it on your piece of land, not on mine." And then to distract him she smiled at him, a dazzling bright smile. "But I will make you tea. I make very good tea."

"Tea for ladies, or tea for a man?"

Her lips curved. "I'm sure I can manage to make a manly cup. So take your coat off and please have a seat by my fire."

They spent the next hour sipping tea and sharing toasted bread.

It was the simplest of meals and yet to McKenna it felt like a feast. It was *so* nice having company. There were a lot of things she'd missed since arriving in Emigrant last August, but the dearth of company was the worst.

There were so many nights when she longed to hear another voice. So any nights when she longed for someone to sit across from her and just look up sometimes and give her a smile—

As Sinclair had done just now.

A ripple of pleasure coursed through her. She loved his smiles. She loved him.

It was suddenly very quiet, and the quiet became increasingly intimate. Her body warmed and her lips felt sensitive. "More tea?" she asked huskily.

He shook his head. "I'm good. And you do make a manly cup. Thank you."

"Thank you for fixing my stove's chimney."

His blue eyes held hers. "Not your stove," he teased soft-ly, a warmth in his deep voice that reminded her of nights long ago when he'd been there at her side during the darkest point she'd known.

He hadn't been afraid of her grief.

He hadn't been afraid to let her feel.

He'd just loved her through it all.

Her eyes burned and her chest seized. He'd been her rock. He'd kept her stable and strong.

No wonder she'd turned to him, for comfort. And then the comfort became passion, and their first kiss had turned her world upside down.

Each evening the goodnight kiss became longer, the de-sire growing hotter, but he never let it go too far. Sinclair had integrity. He showed restraint, respect, determined to protect her reputation.

Awareness crackled between them now, the energy be-tween them nearly as bright as the fire. She wanted him to kiss her again. She wanted to know if his kisses would still melt her. She suspected they would...

McKenna forced herself to speak. "How do you know how to fix everything?" she asked, her voice soft and unusu-ally breathy.

He knew, she thought. He knew how he was affecting her. She wasn't surprised. He knew her so well.

His blue gaze held hers. "How do you know how to teach math and science and reading?"

She felt his scrutiny all the way through her. "You learn how."

"Exactly."

Her head spun. Dizzy, she drew a slow breath. "What about when you left school for the mines? Wasn't that quite difficult? You weren't even sixteen yet."

"Do you really want to talk about me working in the mines?"

"You've never said much to me about those years."

"Those were long years."

"So tell me about them. Tell me about you. Weren't you scared when you went to work underground the first time?"

The fire cast a gold flickering light over his profile. "I don't know if I was scared. But I didn't like it. I also didn't have a choice. It was my job."

And he always did what he was supposed to do. He was that man. He was that dependable.

Her chest grew tight. She exhaled slowly. "If I were your mother I wouldn't have wanted you down there."

"If you were my mother, you'd be grateful I had a job. She was grieving my dad and afraid of losing the house. I kept the roof over our heads. We were all grateful for that."

She felt sudden shame. She had no worries compared to him.

He must have read her discomfort because he smiled

crookedly. "It wasn't all bad. I made friends, and we looked out for each other. They became my second family."

"Was everyone that close?"

"I think it depended on your shift, and your team, and how they treated you. The men I worked with knew my dad, and they adopted me, just as later I adopted the younger lads when they hired on."

"Hopefully there weren't that many young boys down in the mines."

He shifted, extended his legs, one boot over the other. "Do you know how the copper is mined? Do you know anything about a miner's life?"

"I read things, newspaper articles and so forth, but you never said anything and my father never talked about it at all."

"I deliberately said little, wanting to shield you as much as I could from the reality."

"Why?"

He hesitated. "I don't think you have any idea how hard men really do work. Not men like your father, but rather, the men employed in his mines to provide you with the luxuries you took for granted."

She winced. "Ouch."

"You were innocent. I wanted to protect you. And I suppose I wanted to be like your father, and keep you from knowing what the world was really like."

"I know the rudimentary facts of mining. The objective

being to follow the ore vein and get the ore to the surface. I know that in Father's larger mines, he had bigger equipment, and in the smaller mines, his men would use more hand tools, along with a bucket and small steam hoist for carrying both the laboring men and ore to the surface."

"Those laboring men. Do you know anything about their shift? Did you know they had daily and weekly quotas?"

She shook her head.

"Those men—"

"Men like you," she interrupted.

"They worked ten hours a day, seven days a week. Most of the men I worked with in Butte worked twenty-six to twenty-eight days a month. The only time we received time off was if big equipment needed repair. Most workers couldn't even take time off for Sundays. I did, but I was an exception to the rule as my father was gone and the foreman knew I was the only man left in my family."

She just looked at him.

"We started work at seven am and, after changing into work clothes, we'd gather around the shaft collar and wait for our bucket down. The bucket wasn't very big—it could hold just two or three of us at a time—and we'd be lowered into the shaft by the hoist. Every couple of weeks the bucket would come crashing down, or tipping and miners would fall three hundred feet to three thousand feet down. We'd lose miners regularly in those buckets. You always said a prayer before you went down, knowing one of these days it'd be your turn and you'd never make it back up." He paused, studied her face. "Have you heard enough?"

She had, but she wouldn't tell him. "No."

"Once you arrived at your work level, you'd leave your station and head into the drift—a tunnel that follows the ore—and your only light is a torch or candle. It was dark as hell and smelled damp and felt like a grave. Every single day. For ten hours a day. Seven days a week."

"When I first started, I was a mucker. It's the lowest of the low jobs. Anyone can muck. It's just shoveling waste or ore down a chute. And then gradually I worked up to tramming, and blasting. Like most men in Butte, I was paid by the amount of rock I was able to send up to the surface each day. You get the ore out by drilling holes six to eight feet deep in the granite, and then filling the holes with dynamite. You drill the holes by hand with a partner. One of you turns the steel and the other has the sledge. I was the one with the sledge. Why? Because I was the biggest and one of the strongest and I could hammer at granite all day, ten hours a day, six and seven days a week."

"Sinclair," she whispered, her chest squeezing tight, pain filling her.

"I never told you that the tunnels were sometimes so low that I could never stand straight. I never told you that I spent virtually my entire day in darkness, leaving the shaft only when night had fallen. I never told you that the temperatures would get so high we'd have to strip—daily—to our waists because it was as hot as the desert in summer. Suffocatingly hot, and humid, the air so thick that you couldn't breathe. You'd feel as if you were choking to death on the moisture and dust."

She looked away, eyes burning.

"As Johanna told you, my father died from the dust. The dust kills men eventually. You can only work down there so long before your lungs fail." He was silent a long moment. "That's why my goal from the beginning was getting promoted. I had to prove that I was better than the others, and that I didn't just work harder, but I worked smarter. I didn't want to spend my life underground. I wanted to be one of those foremen on the surface, and that was just the first step."

"You succeeded."

"I did. I became a foreman on the outside, and then I came here as the superintendent. And I owe my success to you."

"Me? How?"

"You gave me purpose, and meaning. And even though I did it for you, it was also good for me."

IT WAS TRUE, he thought, looking at her. She'd changed his life for the better.

He'd enjoyed tonight, too. It was an almost perfect

night. He didn't want it to end.

How could life be better then this?

He had a fire and good conversation and the company of a beautiful woman, and not just any beautiful woman, but his.

When McKenna smiled, she glowed, her face lighting up, her eyes sparkling. She'd had the same mischievous sparkle as a girl. Her eyes were the things he remembered best. Her eyes were what caught his attention. He'd turn his head and discover her watching him with those dark, curious eyes and then he'd wink at her and she'd just shine.

Not many women shined the way she did.

He didn't know at what point his protective instincts turned to love, but one day he looked at her and realized she was it. She was the one for him. And from then on he lived for her, knowing he'd give up everything for her. That he'd do anything to defend her. That she was his heart and soul.

"I should go," he said gruffly, getting to his feet.

"Must you? It's not that late," she answered even as she rose.

"I'm sure my horse would argue that point."

She laughed and he felt as if she'd just rewarded him with a prize. Her smiles were rare and she didn't laugh enough these days.

She needed a man to make her smile, a man who understood that her laughter was like rain to thirsty fields. She needed to laugh, and laugh often.

"What are you doing for Thanksgiving?" he asked.

"I think the Hoffmans—"

"Not the Hoffmans again."

"They are very kind to me."

"Fine. But let me be kind to you, too. Join us for Thanksgiving. I will pick you up on the way."

She gave him a long look. "That does not sound like much of a holiday for anyone."

"There's no feud with my family."

"Ha!"

"They care about you. And they know I care about you. They also know I'm not going to dinner if you don't come. I'm not going to leave you alone on Thanksgiving—" He held up a hand, stopping her. "And the Hoffmans can barely feed all those boys, so politely decline their offer and join me instead."

She gave her head a slight shake and yet she was smiling. "I'm not your problem."

"Well, apparently you are, until I see you settled."

"I am settled."

"I mean, married."

She groaned. "That's not happening. Marriage is not for me. So prepare yourself for years of fussing over my well-being. Decades, Sinclair."

"Decades, you say?"

"Mmmm. Decades of caring for your spinster friend from Butte."

He reached past her, lifting his heavy coat and hat from the hook by the door. His arm brushed her shoulder, accidentally skimming the softness of her breast. His body hardened in response, hunger surging within him.

He hated leaving her. It went against everything in him.

"I'll be here Thanksgiving midmorning," he said tautly, opening the door.

She followed him out. "What can I bring? Some of my delicious bread?"

He grimaced. "No need. Save that delicious bread for yourself." And then he closed the distance and placed a light, chaste kiss on her forehead. "Good night, Mac."

Her lips curved, her expression wistful. "Good night, Sin."

"Lock the door behind me."

"I will."

"Do it now, so I can rest easy."

She looked at him for a moment, emotion filling her eyes and it was all he could do not to take her in his arms and kiss her the way he wanted to.

His woman. His.

And then she was stepping back into the cabin and the door shut. He heard the heavy bolt slide, and felt the weight of it from his heart to his gut. It was so damn hard to leave her.

CHAPTER ELEVEN

M cKENNA WAS GLAD she'd dressed in her best choco- late silk and mocha velvet dress when they reached downtown Marietta and she discovered that Thanksgiving dinner wasn't at Mrs. Douglas' flat, but the Graff Hotel's handsome dining room with its beamed ceiling, green walls, and tall pots filled with orchids and ferns.

Sinclair had organized the dinner and they were a table of nine as the Brambles and the Burnetts had been invited as Sinclair's guests, too.

Mr. Graff, the owner of the hotel, worked the dining room during the meal, checking on every table's satisfaction and comfort. McKenna had never met the German before but liked him immediately; particularly when she discovered his menu had been inspired by the menu being served to the president in Washington. Stuffed turkey and goose and prime rib. Three kinds of potatoes, string beans, cauliflower au gratin, and stewed tomatoes, with Chickasaw pudding and pies and ice creams for dessert. There were also maca- roons and merengue and cakes with fresh brewed smyra coffee.

McKenna was grateful she was seated by Mrs. Bramble, and away from Johanna and Ellie Burnett, but she felt Ellie's gaze during the meal, Ellie's expression increasingly speculative.

During dinner, there was a toast to the late president, Abraham Lincoln, for making Thanksgiving a national holiday. Mr. Burnett, a tall, rangy Texan, rose and proposed a toast to Sinclair Douglas for his generosity and friendship, thanking him for bringing them all together today.

McKenna looked down the table and her eyes met Sinclair's and held. She slowly smiled and he smiled back and in that moment there was no one else there. It was just them, Sinclair and McKenna, against the world. It was as it had always been, as teenagers in Butte, as young adults writing letters. It was them with their hopes and dreams.

Sinclair and McKenna together and it was perfect.

He was perfect.

He was.

Late that afternoon after saying goodbye to everyone, they walked, just the two of them, from the Graff to the courthouse, wandering through the public gardens. They walked until the sun dropped behind the mountains and the lavender light of dusk spread over the town.

"We should head back home before it gets too late," he said.

She nodded, and they returned to the hotel for his vehicle.

As he drove, she sat close. They didn't talk much, but the silence was almost like a conversation. Utterly content, McKenna felt her hip against his, and she tucked her hand deeper into the crook of his arm.

He made her feel safe. He made her feel so good.

"How do you do it?" she murmured, lifting her head to look up at the white moon.

He looked at her, eyebrow lifting.

"You make the ordinary extraordinary," she said. "You make the whole world come alive."

"It is alive. You just have to pay attention."

Her gaze met his. "I am now."

For a moment there was silence, and then his head dipped, blocking the moon. His lips brushed hers, letting her feel his breath and the coolness of his mouth on hers.

She shivered at the sensation, pleasure and surprise making her tingle all over.

"Easy," he murmured, as her breath hitched and she shuddered again. "It's just me, sweetheart." His hands were at her neck, and then beneath her hair, tilting her head back so he could deepen the kiss.

Her hands went to his chest to steady herself, but the moment she touched him, she wanted more. She slid her hands beneath his coat to find the warm, hard planes of his chest. He felt so good and she leaned in closer.

The kiss was as overwhelming as her feelings. She gave him her heart all over again. Love was murky and intense, baffling and consuming, but loving him wasn't even a choice. Loving him was like breathing. She did it without thinking.

Eventually the kiss ended, but she kept her hand tucked inside his coat, feeling his heart beat.

When they reached her house she reluctantly drew away. He helped her out of his buggy and walked her up the porch, entering the cabin first to be sure she was safe.

She was. She was with him.

She flew in the clouds and he was her rock, her foundation and earth.

"Good night," he said, head lowering to kiss her again.

She clung to him, head spinning, heart beating. When he finally lifted his head she saw stars. "Good night, Sin," she whispered, smiling up at him. "That was one of my favorite Thanksgivings ever."

"I'm glad you joined us. I hope you know you have friends here, McKenna."

"I know that you are my friend here."

"You belong here. Don't ever forget that."

McKenna spent Friday reading and writing letters, and then on Saturday she walked to Bottler's in Emigrant to mail her letters to Amelia and Mary. There was no mail for her today and so she finished her shopping and thanked the clerk and headed out.

She'd just started walking when she heard a woman call her name.

McKenna turned to discover Ellie Burnett seated in a glossy black buggy drawn by a matching black horse. Ellie wore a dark gray wool coat with black velvet trim, her large, elegant hat pinned at an angle on her gleaming red hair.

She looked impossibly pretty and polished, and McKenna couldn't help wishing she'd made more of an effort this morning.

Ellie lifted a hand, gesturing for McKenna to join her.

McKenna shifted her heavy bag with potatoes and turnips, soap and sundry to her other arm. "Good afternoon, Miss Burnett."

"Good afternoon, Miss Frasier. Wasn't that a lovely Thanksgiving dinner?"

"It was," McKenna agreed. "The Graff does a splendid job."

"Indeed it does. Can I give you a ride home?" Ellie smiled. "I'm heading into Marietta, and would be happy to drop you off on the way."

"Thank you for the kind offer, but I don't mind walking. The exercise is good for me. It's about the only exercise I get these days."

"I'm sure that's not true. You have to chop wood and fetch water and clean the school every week."

"The students help me with much of that. They're very good to me."

"Yes, like the Hoffmans taking you to town with them." She smiled and patted the bench seat. "Join me. You're about to drop whatever it is you're carrying and there is no point in walking when I can get you back much faster, leaving you more time to tackle all those chores waiting for you. Besides, it's threatening to rain and you don't want to have to deal with the mud on top of everything else."

Ellie Burnett's tone set McKenna's teeth on edge but she didn't want to offend Johanna's friend. Besides, dark clouds were gathering over Emigrant peak. Rain probably wasn't that far off.

"True," McKenna replied. "And thank you. I'd be delighted to join you."

She climbed into the buggy and placed her bag at her feet and then they were off at a brisk pace. McKenna didn't want to be impressed by Ellie's skillful driving but Ellie had excellent command of her spirited horse.

For several minutes they discussed pleasantries—weather, upcoming holidays, the various bills the new state government was trying to put through before the end of the year—and then Ellie shifted the conversation, almost as deftly as she steered the horse around a fallen tree nearly blocking the road.

"You surprise me," Ellie said with a glance at McKenna. "You have a very good grasp of politics and business."

"I owe that to my father. He used to discuss both with me."

"Mine, too. What would we do without our fathers?"

McKenna couldn't answer that and for several minutes they lapsed into silence and then Ellie broke the quiet. "Are you pleased with your position at the school here? Or do you find it inferior due to your education?"

"Not at all. It's been a good challenge."

"So you don't intend to leave anytime soon?"

"Absolutely not." McKenna's attention was drawn to a fragmented boulder scattered across the road ahead, but Ellie handled the rock and her horse with the same confidence she'd handled the fallen tree. "I intend to be here for quite a long time."

"No plans to marry anytime soon?"

"No."

"Why not?"

McKenna couldn't quite suppress her shudder. "I'm not the marrying kind."

Ellie glanced at her from beneath the brim of her hat, brow arched. "That surprises me."

"Why?"

"Forgive me if this isn't my place, but people are talking." She paused, creating a delicate tension. "They're aware of the extraordinary amount of time you and Mr. Douglas spend together. It's widely assumed that you two have a…liaison?"

McKenna stiffened. "Who says that?"

"More people than you might think."

"I don't believe it. No. There's no reason for speculation, either."

"You must admit you've spent considerable time together. *Alone.*" Ellie glanced at her, her expression blank, and suddenly impossible to read. "It's one thing for him to drive you home from a party, but another to purchase and install a stove in your home—"

"The stove isn't for me, it's for the school, and for future teachers."

"I'm just not sure the superintendent would see it that way. Mr. Egan is quite conservative. His teachers must be above reproach."

"I have known Mr. Douglas since we were children."

"But you're not a child anymore, are you, Miss Frasier? And I do believe Mr. Egan was giving you a second chance by hiring you for Park County's little school. He believed you were reformed—"

"Reformed?"

"That you'd put your scandalous behavior behind you."

McKenna's lips pressed together. She was too insulted to speak.

Ellie shrugged lightly. "I see that I've upset you, but what kind of a friend would I be if I didn't warn you that members of the community have noted your indiscretions, and are uncomfortable with your lack of propriety? I will try to intercede on your behalf, Miss Frasier, and beg them not to write Mr. Egan just yet, but I need assurance from you that you will not continue encouraging Mr. Douglas. At least, not if you desire to retain your current job at the school in Emigrant."

"I'd like to walk." McKenna choked, reaching for the bag at her feet. "Please pull over. I'd like to get out now."

"But we're almost to your turn off."

"We've another mile, at least, and I'd prefer to walk the rest of the way."

"You're not angry with me, are you?" Ellie slowed her horse, then brought him to a complete stop. "I would think you'd appreciate someone being honest with you. You don't want to spend your entire life alienated from others, do you?"

McKenna felt so very much in that moment—fury, outrage, shame—it was difficult to know which words to say. "I wish I could trust you, Miss Burnett. Alas, I do not know your heart, or your intentions."

"They are but the purest."

"How lucky for me then, that you have chosen to befriend me. Good day." McKenna stepped out of the buggy and started walking.

Ellie drew the buggy alongside McKenna's. "I don't blame you entirely, Miss Frasier. How could I when Mr. Douglas has encouraged your dependence? But that must be nipped in the bud. You are not the one for him—"

"But you are?" McKenna spun on her heel, and faced Ellie, temper barely leashed. "Is that what you believe?"

"I know I would never abuse him as you have. I would never dream of playing with his affections. He is the rarest of men. Hardworking, honest, true."

"I do not need you to lecture me about Sin—" She broke off, drew a swift breath. "Mr. Douglas. I know him far better than you."

"Is that so?"

"Yes."

"Then you know it isn't the Hoffmans who send milk and eggs, cheese and butter to you. It's Mr. Douglas. And when you needed a ride into town for the statehood celebrations, it wasn't the Hoffmans who thought of taking you, it was Mr. Douglas' suggestion that they offer to take you." Ellie held up a finger, stopping McKenna. "In case you didn't see the big picture, Mr. Hoffman is Mr. Douglas' ranch foreman. He works for Mr. Douglas, and every egg, or bit of butter or cheese that come to you through those four Hoffman boys, comes not from the Hoffman's generosity, but because Mr. Douglas has provided it. And that, Miss Frasier, would not please Superintendent Egan, either." Then she clucked and gave the reins a shake and continued on, leaving McKenna on the side of the road.

For a long minute McKenna just stood there, too shocked to move. She couldn't believe it. Any of it. And yet she didn't think Ellie Burnett was lying.

Was Sinclair providing for her? Was he sending food through the Hoffmans?

And did everyone truly know that he'd paid her so much attention, or was Miss Burnett just more observant than most?

Did she care more than most?

Or was McKenna's job truly in danger?

The first raindrop fell and McKenna lifted her face to the sky, fighting the emotion threatening to swallow her whole.

How was it possible that she was already the subject of speculation and ugly gossip? Why did everyone assume the worst of her?

In New York last spring *Town Topics* named McKenna the most scandalous woman of the year, and now here she was in tiny little Emigrant about to lose everything. Over a man. Again.

More raindrops fell. McKenna began walking quickly, not wanting to get soaked by the freezing rain. The last thing she needed was to get sick.

The sound of a horse behind her made her move closer to the side of the road. She glanced behind her as the horse and rider approached and then nearly screamed in frustration. Of course it'd be Sinclair. Who else?

She put her head down and began walking more quickly, as if she could somehow make herself invisible. But of course he knew it was her, and he slowed his horse.

She hunched her shoulders as he stopped next to her.

"Give me your hand, I'll pull you up in front of me," he said.

"I'm almost home," she said, trying to ignore the stitch in her side from walking so fast.

"You're more than a half mile away and it's going to come down hard. Give me your hand—"

"No, thank you. I needed the exercise."

"It's raining, McKenna."

"I like the rain, and I'm glad for the rain. Mr. Bottler and Mr. Stickland's crops needed it."

"They've harvested their crops for the winter."

"Then it's good for their livestock."

"And it's good for you, yes?"

"Yes." Her voice shook. She was so upset, not just with him, but with all of them. "There's nothing like a walk in the rain."

"Especially when it turns your path to mud."

"I like the mud."

"No, you don't."

"Go away." She choked, the rain beginning to come down harder, pelting her face and hat, making her bag of potatoes and turnips even heavier. She shifted the bag from one arm to another, trying to keep her arm from going numb. "Your help is not needed."

"Something has happened."

"Of course something has happened! I'm the most scandalous woman in America!"

"I did think *Town Topics* laid it on a bit heavy. You're fallen, yes, but I don't think you've quite earned the title of most scandalous woman. I am sure there are a few women whose behavior is worse."

"Is that a joke? Very nice." She wiped an arm across her face trying to dry it even as the rain kept falling. "Humor is so good for lifting the spirits."

"Lift your hem. Your skirt is dragging in the mud."

"Excellent. That will be delightful to wash."

"You are having a tantrum."

"No. I'm just working very hard not to say what I want to say."

"Which is?"

"Please, Sinclair, *go*. Go before someone else sees us, and spreads more gossip, fueling speculation that you and I are having a torrid affair—"

"Is that Miss Burnett said?"

She shot him a furious glance, angry, so angry with him. "How did you know I rode with her?"

"I was at the saloon across from Bottler's store. I saw you leave with her."

"So why are you here? Why aren't you at the saloon still? Or do you like the excitement? Is that why you have the Hoffmans bringing me food? Is it beneficial to you somehow, having everyone gossip?" Her bag slipped and she jerked to catch it but the strings had loosened and a potato rolled out. She bent to pick up the potato but another spilled and then the turnips, falling into the mushy soil.

She let out a scream of vexation and Sinclair was dismounting and there beside her, crouching in the mud, picking up root vegetables and shoving them into the bag before tying the bag to his saddle.

Without asking her permission, he wrapped his hands around her waist and lifted her onto the horse as if she weighed no more than the sack of potatoes. He slid a foot into the stirrup and swung into the saddle, and pulled her against him as he picked up the reins, and spurred the horse to a trot.

McKenna sat tall, trying not to lean against Sinclair, which proved nearly impossible with the jogging motion of the horse. She'd bounced and bumped against him her hands flailing until she grabbed a handful of the horse's mane and tried to pull away from Sinclair's hard thighs and broad chest.

"Can we please walk?" she gritted. "I'm about to fall off!"

"I won't let you fall."

His arm tightened around her waist, his hand flat against her belly. Heat rushed through her, the heat coming in waves until she felt as if she'd pop out of her skin.

"I can't breathe," she said, drawing away.

He eased his hold and she was able to lean forward a few inches, but she was still so aware of him behind her, her body tingling from head to foot. But it wasn't just her senses that were stirred. She felt an overwhelming awareness of him, and life, and who they'd been as well as whom they were now.

She wasn't supposed to still care this much for him. She

wasn't supposed to feel the way she did about him.

"You smell like sheepskin," she said huskily, fighting the intensity of her emotions.

"You smell like wet wool."

"I love that smell."

He laughed softly, a deep rumble in his chest that she could feel all the way through her.

She wanted his arms tighter. She wanted him to hold her closer. She wanted all the things she'd never had with him… or anyone else.

McKenna blinked, clearing the salty sting from her eyes, and drew a deep breath, dangerously close to breaking down. "I'm afraid I'm going to lose my job."

"I'll speak to her."

"Do you think she'd listen?"

"I would hope so. I'm friends with her father. I've known her since she was sixteen."

"She wants you," MeKenna said after a moment. "And your family wants her for you, too."

He said nothing.

"They said they hope you'll be married soon."

His shoulders shifted. "Nobody chooses my bride for me."

"You want to marry?"

"Yes. I've always wanted a family. I've worked hard so I can provide for my family." His voice hardened. "You're the one that doesn't like marriage. Not me."

"I didn't say I disliked marriage. I just said I didn't trust... men, and therefore marriage."

"Maybe I should just propose to Miss Burnett," he said flatly, his voice low.

But she heard him, and she straightened abruptly, shoulders squaring as she tried to glance back at him, but Sinclair was so much taller than her and with his hat on she couldn't see his features well enough to read his expression.

They didn't speak again the rest of the ride home.

Once in front of her cabin, he lowered her down from the saddle, and handed her the cloth shopping bag.

"That was oh, so very low," she said tersely, stepping up onto her small covered porch. "And absolutely unnecessary. Why threaten me with Miss Burnett?"

He was off his horse and following her up the steps. "Not threatening you. I'm just telling you how I feel—"

"You want her?"

"I want you, but for reasons I don't understand I can't have you. Not then, not now."

"I haven't even been here five months. I can't quit teaching now. I need to think of my students, and I need to think about what's best for me."

"For you."

"Sinclair, this is how I make my living. It's how I take care of myself."

"You know I could take care of you."

"And what if you changed your mind? What if you

walked out on me?"

"I would never do that."

"How do I know? My father—"

"I am not your father." He stiffened, offended. "I am not your Bernard. And if you do not know that by now, if you do not trust me by now, then you will never trust me."

"It's not you I don't trust. It's *me*!"

He caught her to him, and kissed her fiercely, his hands cupping her face, tilting her head back to take her mouth with hunger and anger and desperation.

He tasted of love and passion and desperation.

She heard a warning voice in her head. The voice wasn't quiet, either. Things were changing. They'd reached the breaking point, and if they weren't careful, it'd be a point of no return.

Whatever happened now…

Whatever happened next…

Sinclair pressed her back against the cabin's roughhewn wall, his big body trapping her. "Tell me you want me," he said, his hands braced on either side of her head, his this moving between hers. "Tell me."

"I do—Sinclair, I do, but I can't."

"Can't?"

"Can't give you what you want."

"Why not?"

"I need to do something right. I need to do something well, and this job is my chance to do something well."

"So you won't have me?" he said, stepping away from her, hands falling to his sides.

She caught at his arm, keeping him from moving further away. "Please, Sinclair, listen to me—"

"I have," he snapped. "That's all I've been doing for weeks. Listening and asking questions and listening some more but it's always about you. What you want, what you fear, what you need."

"Because you *asked* me."

"Why don't you ask me what I want, and fear, and need? Why don't I matter as much as you?"

She felt a lump fill her throat, matching the weight in her stomach.

"Is it because I'm a Douglas from Dublin Gulch? Is it because I don't represent power in your world? Why would you give Bernard everything and yet withhold it from me?"

"I didn't give him *everything*."

"No? Are you still pure then?"

Her heart fell, and she went cold all over. "Is my innocence so very important to you?"

"I respected you. I kept you chaste."

She couldn't breathe. She hurt all over. She knew what he was asking. She knew what he wanted to hear.

This would be the time to tell him she was still a virgin. This would be the time to explain, but he was enraged and she didn't know how to manage Sinclair now.

"My innocence is no one's business but mine," she said.

"I do not belong to you. Nor do I owe you any explanation."

"You are so spoiled. You were raised to think that you are the sun, and the rest of the world just exists to revolve around you, enjoying your warmth and light, *when* you choose to radiate heat and light."

"Wrong!" she cried, flinging the word at him as if it were a knife. "I wasn't raised to think of myself that way, and maybe I was spoiled—indulged by my father as so many fathers indulge their daughters—but I never thought of myself as the center of the universe until *you* turned me into the sun, big and bright, filled with life. If you're not happy that I have such confidence, blame yourself, because you made me this way."

"Me?"

"Yes, you! You, with all your ridiculous love!" She was practically shouting the words, absolutely beside herself because he couldn't see that she was his, and had always been his, and would always be his. Twenty-five years... fifty years from now. It didn't matter. The time apart wouldn't matter, either. She'd always love him. She'd always be his, and he'd be hers. For better, or worse. And maybe they couldn't make it work in their lifetime but it didn't change the love. It had been there in the beginning and it would be there at the end. "Now make the gossip stop. It has to stop. I need my job."

He walked to his horse and reached for the reins. "You had other choices, McKenna. You didn't have to live like this."

"I could have married, yes? I could have let a man take care of me."

"Is that so bad?"

"I don't want to be totally dependent on anyone."

"I am not anyone. I have loved you for half my life, McKenna. If I am just anyone, it's time for this to end."

"That's not what I meant," she said. "That's not what I was saying. You're taking my words and twisting them—"

"Marry me, next month."

"*Sinclair.*"

"You won't, will you?"

"Does it have to be now? Can't we wait? Let me finish the year and see how things are this summer?"

Sinclair ground his teeth, his hard jaw jutting.

For a long minute, he was silent, and then he shook his head and crossed to his horse, and put a foot in the stirrup, then seated himself. "I'll make the gossip stop."

He turned the horse around and she hurried down the steps, running to catch up with him. "No goodbye? Is that it?"

He glanced down at her, blue gaze cold. "Goodbye," he said grimly.

She grabbed at his calf. "Not like that, Sinclair!"

He made a rough sound. "You win, Mac. I'm giving you what you want."

"And what is that?"

"Your freedom." Then he spurred the horse and he was

off, cantering across the field.

HIS RIDICULOUS LOVE.

Her words kept ringing in his head, sharp and mocking. Her eyes had been bright and hard as she'd flung his ridiculous love in his face.

Once he reached the main road, Sinclair let his horse go, the canter becoming a gallop, anger rushing through him, making him see red.

Why did he keep seeking her out? What did he want from her? What did he expect?

That she might have changed? That life and the challenges she faced had opened her eyes?

It seemed he was wrong.

It seemed he would always be wrong about her.

His frustration was huge. It flamed his anger and the old pain, making him want to hurt something, break something, break her—

No.

Not break her.

He just had to avoid her.

She wasn't good for him. She made him insane. And surely after fourteen years, he'd had enough of the Frasiers?

Surely after fourteen years, he could focus on someone else. Create a new future.

He had much to offer. Stability, security, protection,

companionship. He'd be a good husband, an excellent provider, and a devoted father. And once he was committed, he wouldn't stray, either. He would never do that to his wife. It was the worst betrayal he could think of.

Maybe it was time to think seriously on marriage.

And if he was serious about marrying, why wait? He'd be thirty in May. He had a fine two-story house with a big bed in an upstairs bedroom that featured a high sloped ceiling and a dormer window where one could see the moon.

He slept in that bed, in that room, alone. He'd lived in his fine house for two years alone. Why spend another long winter by himself? There was no reason to remain a bachelor when he could take a Christmas wife.

Ellie Burnet was young and beautiful, healthy and strong. She knew his life, too. She'd understand what needed to be done. She'd helped her father with his work. She would be a good partner, a suitable mate.

Maybe Ellie had done him a favor today, threatening to report McKenna to Superintendent Egan.

Maybe she'd forced his hand, and normally he didn't like to be pressured, but when it came to McKenna, he was a fool. Maybe he needed the push to make him see what he'd refused to see—McKenna Frasier would never pick him.

He spurred his horse faster. They galloped, the wind whistling as he leaned close over the stallion's neck.

He felt dangerous and wild. Wild with frustration and humiliation and most painful of all, grief.

He was letting her go.

He was done. There was no more room for her in his heart, or in his life.

CHAPTER TWELVE

H E WAS ENGAGED.

McKenna was at school when she found out, one of the Hoffman boys pushing past one of his brothers to get to her first to break the news.

They all thought it was a great story. They were excited by the news. Mr. Douglas, the strapping miner who'd become a big rancher, was marrying the Texan's only daughter.

The children talked about it all day, and then all week as they learned new details. Mr. Burnett was throwing an engagement party at the Graff in their honor. It would be a holiday party, no, a Christmas ball, a *lavish* Christmas ball and there would be a band from Butte, and an entire table of cakes, and lots of beer and wine and champagne, the champagne coming in by train from New York.

The children shared too much of what their parents said at home. Some parents were invited, but not everyone because it was a formal dinner with five—no, seven—courses, and even though the ballroom was huge, Mr. Burnett wanted to keep it intimate, which was why he was only including his friends.

Mrs. Douglas and Miss Douglas were inviting friends, too. They were inviting more than just a few friends. They were so happy for Mr. Douglas. It was a dream come true and because it was the biggest party of the year, Miss Douglas was sewing many splendid gowns for the ladies attending the party on Saturday, December twenty-first.

McKenna was glad she didn't receive an invite for this party. She said those exact words when Jillian Parker came to call on her a week before the school ended for Christmas vacation.

"You might change your mind when you see this," Jillian answered, drawing a heavy envelope from her bag and handing it to her. "Your very own invitation."

McKenna held the envelope in her hands, heartsick.

She didn't get invited to the Brambles' party when she wanted to go last October, and when she didn't want to attend a party, the invitation arrived early.

"What do you think of the match?" Jillian asked, going to sit by the fire.

McKenna's hands shook as she poured the hot water for their tea. "I haven't an opinion."

"Everyone says it's a good match as Mr. Douglas runs cattle on his land, just like Mr. Burnett does. Their property isn't far, either, so Miss Burnett will remain close to her father."

"It sounds as if everyone knows best," McKenna answered, carrying the cups to the fireplace. She thought she'd come to terms with the engagement news but suddenly she felt heartbroken all over again.

It was impossible, absolutely impossible, to imagine a future without Sinclair.

And once Jillian left, McKenna sank onto her bed, and buried her face in her pillow, howling into the soft down, unable to contain her sorrow.

Not Sinclair and Ellie. Not Sinclair and Ellie. Not Sinclair and anyone. Sinclair was hers.

THANK GOD IT was weekend.

McKenna was so heartsick she could barely function. After Jillian had left yesterday, McKenna had more or less stayed in bed, and she'd only gotten up today to do the most necessary chores.

But every little task made her want to cry.

What had she done?

She couldn't live without him. She couldn't even go a week without him. It was just eight days since he'd left her, and it felt like forever. Maybe because in those eight days, he'd gone straight to Ellie and proposed and her father had immediately planned a party that promised to be the party of all parties.

THE SNOW BEGAN to fall steadily Sunday afternoon. It snowed all night and when Sinclair woke up the next morning, the fat thick white flakes were still coming down, turning the valley into a sea of white.

After moving his horses and cattle into the barn and making sure they had plenty of feed and water, he returned to his house and stared out the window facing Emigrant Peak, the mountain completely obscured by clouds.

It was cold and growing colder. The national weather were now predicting a winter much like last year with its record cold fronts and blizzards and snow piling fifteen, twenty feet high or more.

He knew how to survive in the cold. He knew his limits, he'd been tested over the years and he understood when to stay in, and when to venture out, and how to handle nature at its worst. But McKenna didn't.

She was woefully unprepared.

And, no, she wasn't his anymore. He was committed elsewhere, engaged to Ellie, but that didn't mean he wanted McKenna to be hurt, or suffer.

Watching the snow fall in a blinding sheet of white, he worried.

THE SNOW JUST kept falling.

It had started yesterday, Sunday afternoon and now it was knee deep. McKenna didn't expect any students but at the same time she wasn't sure if any would try to make it.

She dressed and trudged through the thick fluffy snow, batting away the flakes when they landed beneath her bonnet. Once inside the freezing school, she lit a fire and changed the date on the blackboard and with a trembling hand she wrote the morning lessons on the board before going outside to shovel a path for students.

There was a great deal of snow and it took a great deal of effort to clear even a partial path. She worked for an hour and when no students appeared, she realized that it was unlikely anyone was coming.

McKenna put out the fire, closed the school, and returned home, her boots soaked through and her hair quite damp despite the hat she'd worn. Inside her own cabin, McKenna was grateful for her new stove, as it proved particularly useful for drying wet shoes and coats and heating the water to warm her chilled hands and feet.

It stopped snowing in the night, and in the morning the landscape she knew was gone, everything utterly still and a pure, glistening white.

Again, McKenna dressed and headed for school, not at all sure what the conditions were like in the rest of the valley. She sank into the snow, hip high in places, and it took her a long time to go a very short distance.

She hoped her students were staying home. She wished she'd stayed home. But once at school she built the fire, and then shoveled off the steps, and then tried to clear a path, but her efforts halfhearted because she was freezing cold and soaked through.

McKenna knelt next to the biggest potbelly stove, hands up, teeth chattering, unable to get warm.

She shouldn't have come today. She should have known that no one was coming. She should have known so many things that she didn't.

One day she'd get it together.

One day she'd amazed everyone... maybe even amaze herself.

The minutes ticked by. She couldn't move. There was no point in moving. It would only mean crossing the field to get to her house. She didn't feel much like dealing with the snow.

McKenna rested her head on her arm, and closed her eyes, letting the fire warm her. Her thoughts drifted. She found herself thinking of Sinclair. Her favorite person. Always her favorite person.

But she'd blown it. She'd been too weak, too afraid.

If she were a true Christian, she'd be happy for Sinclair, happy he'd found his match, someone who respected him, someone who would be there for him.

Ellie knew the ranching business. She knew all about cattle. She'd be a great help for him, whereas McKenna knew nothing about cattle or ranching. She knew nothing about being a rancher's wife.

But she did know Sinclair. She'd always loved Sinclair.

But love wasn't enough. There were still so many obstacles, like their lives and their experiences and their needs that had gone unmet.

McKenna was so lost in thought she didn't hear the door open. But she did hear the thud of boots on the floor, steps heavy.

She sleepily opened her eyes.

Sinclair.

Her heart felt sleepy too, but happy, and she smiled at him, such a tall rugged man covered in white. "Missing a lunch pail?"

"I don't think anyone's coming, sweetheart. Most people are snowed in."

She stretched. "How did you get out then?"

"I'm not most people."

No, he wasn't.

He crossed the floor, walking towards her. "How long have you been sitting there?"

"I don't know. But I'm not as cold as I was."

"You did all that shoveling outside?"

"I wanted to clear a path for the children."

"You should let the boys do that."

"There were no boys here."

"True. But I'm here now. And I'm going to see you back to your house."

"I'm too tired. Let me stay here."

"It's chilly in here. You don't have enough wood. You'll

freeze."

"At least Superintendent Egan will know I was on the job."

He reached down and scooped her up. "We're not having Emigrant's first teacher die on the job."

"You can't carry me back. It's a long walk."

"I walk even further to get to my barn, I think I can manage getting you back."

"I'm heavy."

"And way too talkative." He gave her a crooked smile and she knew he was teasing her. All was okay.

AT HER HOUSE Sinclair built a big fire and refilled her woodbin. He boiled water for tea and once the water boiled he made her a cup and he had one, too. McKenna was unusually quiet as she sat on the side of her bed, a blanket wrapped around her shoulders since she still was chilled.

He couldn't stay much longer. He shouldn't have come in the first place, but at least now he knew she was home and safe, and he could go home and have some peace of mind.

"Thank you," she said, hands clasped around her cup.

He nodded, and followed her gaze. She was looking at the silver framed photo on the mantle. It was a photo of her, and her sister with their father.

"You saved me," she whispered.

He shook his head. "You were fine. You would have been

fine if you'd stayed at school."

"No. I meant when Mother was dying. You saved me. I couldn't have gotten through those last weeks of her life, without you. You kept me whole." She looked at him, dark eyes bright. "But you were right. What have I ever done for you? What have I given you? Just disappointment and pain."

"I'm content with my lot and my life, McKenna."

"I hurt you."

"No more than life hurts one."

She nodded, tears welling, her misery palpable.

He felt a sharp pinch between his ribs. She had no idea how much it hurt him seeing her like this. "Ah, sweetheart," he said softly. "Don't do that." He struggled to smile. "I'm pretty close to forgiving you. Maybe it's time you forgave yourself."

She closed her eyes.

She drew a deep breath, and then another. A tear seeped from beneath her lashes. "It will never be the same, will it?"

The pinch in his chest was sharper, deeper. He shouldn't have come. He hated seeing her like this.

"We had the past," he said roughly. "Maybe we were never meant to have the future."

McKenna drew the blanket over her face, and wept. But even with her head covered, he heard the sobs, low and high at the same time, as if each was being wrenched from her.

Unable to take more, he walked out of the house and stood on the porch, staring blindly at the valley of white.

He couldn't remember seeing her cry since she'd arrived, and now to hear her weep like this, it was hell. He felt like hell. And yet it wasn't his fault.

He'd given her every opportunity to have a life with him, but she hadn't wanted it and he'd grown tired of waiting. He was a patient man but even he had his limits.

Sinclair heard his name being called and then abruptly the door opened and McKenna rushed out. "Wait," she cried, "wait, please."

"I wasn't leaving. I just needed air." He pushed her back inside and closed the door behind him. Barefoot she only reached halfway up his chest. "But I do need to go. I still have all my afternoon chores to do."

She looked like a child wrapped in the blanket, her face pale, cheeks still streaked with tears, her long dark hair spilling over her shoulders.

It would be a death to leave her. But he didn't have a choice. He was committed to Ellie now.

He cleared his throat, battling the emotion, smashing it down. "I can't do this in the future, McKenna. It's not fair to Ellie. Once I'm married, I'm married."

She nodded, eyes huge in her face.

"It's not to hurt you," he added tightly.

"I know," she answered.

"I KNOW," McKENNA repeated hoarsely, struggling to

strengthen her voice. She had to do what was responsible, and proper. For once in her life. "You're right. You can't come back here once you're married."

She wouldn't want him to return, either, not if he was married. Sinclair's integrity mattered to her, and it mattered to the world. His faithfulness had given her strength and hope.

She could still taste her tears and her throat was raw from sobbing but she wouldn't cry again in front of him. It wasn't fair to him.

McKenna squared her shoulders, chin lifting. "Thank you for coming today, to check on me. I'm good now. I promise."

"You know to stay put if there's a blizzard?"

She nodded. "I know that I shouldn't go to school, no."

"And if the blizzard starts when the children are at school?"

"I keep them with me until their parents arrive to collect them."

"What if they cry and beg to go home?"

"I tell them stories and entertain them so they don't cry."

"And what if you're here alone?"

Her lips quivered but she made them smile. "I tell myself stories and entertain myself so I don't cry."

His eyes searched hers. "I will miss you."

He had no idea…

He had no idea at all…

She dug her nails into her palms. "You have been my best friend."

"And you helped me become a man."

"No, that was all you."

"I remember how you'd watch me on the field. Big brown eyes watching every move I'd make."

She fought to hold the tears back. "You were Butte's greatest athlete."

"Is it too late for me to play professional ball?"

She laughed and turned away, quickly brushing the tears from her lashes before he could see. "I am sure you could do anything you set your mind to."

He looked away from her and drew a slow breath.

McKenna knew what was coming next and steeled herself, waiting for it.

"I should go," he said.

It still hurt even though she knew it was coming. "Yes, you should."

"You'll be okay," he said.

"I *am* okay." Because she was. She had to be. "Don't worry about me anymore. I know what I need to do here. I can manage. I promise."

"It's not that easy, though." His deep voice dropped lower. "It's never been easy leaving you, but now—"

"It's time. It's the right thing to do."

He looked at her then, his gaze locking with hers and she said everything with her heart that she couldn't say aloud. *I love you. I will always love you. I will never forget you even if I'm one hundred years old...*

He nearly moved towards her and she stepped back. She couldn't let him come near her. She couldn't be strong if he was close.

"We'll still be friends," she said, retreating to her door and opening it. "We'll always be friends."

He hesitated and then he walked through the door and faced out, the world a stunning pristine white. "Promise?"

Yes. No. "Cross my heart."

He turned to look at her and his mouth curved but his blue eyes weren't smiling. She gave up trying to smile.

"Be careful going home," she said.

He nodded, and then she closed the door, releasing him to the future and the good woman he deserved.

CHAPTER THIRTEEN

McKENNA STARED AT the envelope propped on her mantle, her name written in elegant script. She knew the printed engraved invitation on the square bristol-board by heart, the wording as formal as an invitation she might have received in New York.

Mr. Archibald Burnett requests your company...

McKenna closed her eyes. She should throw the invitation away. She wasn't going to go. It would be disastrous to go. She couldn't bear to see Sinclair with the beautiful Ellie...

She jumped up from her bed and grabbed the invitation from the mantle and tossed it into the fire, letting it burn.

IT WAS FRIDAY and the children were out of school for the next two weeks for their much anticipated Christmas vacation. McKenna scrubbed the chalkboards, and took a broom to the eaves, and then afterwards swept the school house floor before mopping it, getting on her hands and knees to reach every corner.

She worked to keep from thinking about the next two weeks. What would she do without her students? How would she pass the next two weeks alone? How would Christmas be when she was by herself?

And tomorrow was the engagement ball at the Graff.

Of course she wasn't going to go.

She wanted to go.

It would be madness to attend. But McKenna was feeling slightly insane. Her soul mate was marrying someone else.

It was her fault, too. She'd pushed him away with her fear. Jeremy Bernard Clark did more than ruin her reputation. He'd taken her ability to trust.

Finally there was nothing left to clean, and McKenna closed up the school, locking it for the weekend. After bundling up, she walked the short distance to her cabin and opening the door she looked at her life.

The table, the chair, the bed pushed up against the wall. Her stove. The stacked trunks. The lantern and framed photo on the mantle.

This was everything. This was nearly all she owned. She had just a few more treasures she'd kept hidden inside her trunks.

She opened the trunks now and pulled every last thing out.

Her mother's pearls and teardrop earrings. The softest kid gloves Mary had given her for Christmas two years ago. The desk set Sinclair gave her after she'd graduated from

Vassar. A looking glass her father had purchased in Venice for her.

The small pile of books, her five favorite novels. Stories she'd read again and again.

And then her best gowns. The saffron dress she'd worn seven weeks ago to the Brambles' Hallowe'en party, the dark chocolate velvet dress she'd worn for Thanksgiving, a navy and silver silk dress she hadn't worn since leaving New York, and then at the very bottom was her favorite dress of all, the silk a gleaming puddle of red.

It would be the perfect dress for the party at the Graff. She'd look like the heiress she once was, before New York turned their backs on her.

McKenna lifted the crimson ball gown from her trunk and gave the stunning gown a shake and, for a moment, she was back on Fifth Avenue about to enter Mrs. Astor's ballroom.

She wanted to be that person again.

She wanted to be proud and beautiful. She wanted to feel the power of who she was instead of the mouse she'd become.

She'd go. But she needed a ride.

McKenna carefully placed the dress on her bed, and lightly brushed at the silk, trying to smooth wrinkles. But even with wrinkles it was gorgeous and she'd feel like a princess, and maybe it was time to be a princess again, even if just for one night.

Resolved, McKenna pulled on her winter coat and reached for her hat and gloves. If she hurried she could get to and from Emigrant before it was dark. She needed to arrange a ride for the tomorrow night. If she was going to wear her best dress, she needed a proper carriage.

THE GRAND LOBBY of the stately Graff Hotel smelled like a forest, fragrant with pine, and looked like a winter dream, thanks to the massive fir tree filling the center of the marble floor. The soaring tree glittered with silver tinsel, colored glass balls, and one hundred glowing candles.

McKenna stood at the base of the tree, dazzled, transported back to New York, remembering when her father had taken her and Mary to Macy's to see Santa Claus, and the department store's fantastic holiday window displays. How she loved Christmas! And there was nothing like the holidays in New York.

Mr. Graff approached her as she turned from his fine tree. "Do you like it, Miss Frasier?"

"Oh, I do. It makes me so happy. This is such a splendid gift to Marietta."

"I'm not sure if everyone in Marietta approves, but we Germans love our Christmas trees."

"I'm glad, as you do have the best holiday traditions." She smiled, grateful for Mr. Graff. From the beginning, he'd been nothing but kind. "Thank you for sharing with the rest of us." She glanced down the hall leading to the ballroom, her insides suddenly fluttery. "I hear music."

"It's quite a party."

"I can't imagine anyone missing such a special event."

"I'm a little bit surprised you're here." He gave her a pointed look. "When I heard about the engagement I was quite certain that someone had gotten the facts wrong."

She flushed, cheeks hot. "I'm not sure I know what you mean."

"Oh, Miss Frasier, I think you do. Mr. Douglas—"

"I'm very pleased for them," she interrupted breathlessly, hating the sharp pain in her chest, a pain that had lived there ever since she'd found out about the engagement. "They make a handsome couple."

"In that case, if you are happy, I am happy." He bowed and moved on to greet a couple entering the hotel lobby.

SINCLAIR AND ELLIE were making the rounds in the ballroom, speaking to guests, thanking their friends for the well-wishes, when Sinclair heard Ellie draw a sharp breath. He looked up to see what had caught her attention.

McKenna stood in the doorway wearing a gown the color of red wine, her dark hair pinned up with delicate tendrils framing her face. She was breathtaking. No wonder Ellie felt insecure.

Sinclair bent his head, concerned. "Did you not know

she was coming?"

"She was invited," Ellie said shortly. "I just didn't think she would actually show."

"But if you didn't want her here…"

Ellie shook her head. "It doesn't matter. She doesn't matter." Then she turned to smile up into his eyes, her smile dazzling, her gloved hand light on his arm. "It's our night. *Our* celebration."

McKenna was grateful Mrs. Bramble took pity on her, and invited her to sit with her and Mr. Bramble during the meal. Mr. Graff's efficient staff discreetly added a place setting to the Brambles' table for McKenna just before the guests were asked to take their seats.

McKenna had only just sat down in a rustle of silk and satin when a loud shout sounded outside the ballroom. "Douglas! Sinclair Douglas!"

Someone attempted to shush the man but the noise grew louder, more voices, angry shouts, and then the heavy double doors were thrown open.

"Douglas! Where is he?"

There was a shushing of the orchestra. Sinclair rose, dressed in his formal black tie. "I'm here. What is the matter?"

"There's been an accident at the mine. Thirty, forty trapped. Maybe dead."

"How?"

"Explosion, and fire. Most of the men are still down there. Can you help us?"

IT WAS MAYHEM in the ballroom. Men in formal dress ran to collect their coats. Women clustered together, trying to stay out of the way.

Ellie followed Sinclair out of the ballroom to the lobby, pleading with him. "Do not go," she cried, catching his sleeve, holding to his coat. "You cannot go, please!"

"Ellie, I cannot leave those men down there. They are my men—"

"They're not your men! It's not your mine."

"I know that mine. I built that mine. I cannot leave those men to perish."

"It's dangerous!"

"Yes, it is. The living could be suffocating even now."

"Listen to yourself. It's far too dangerous, I can't risk losing you. Let the men who own the mine manage the rescue—"

"You can't seriously be that selfish. Those are family men. Husbands, fathers, brothers."

"And what of your life? Have you thought of that?"

He pulled her hand from his coat. "Yes."

"Sinclair, look at me. Look." She pulled on the lapels of his coat. "You will do those men far more good if you organize the rescue from here. Stay here—"

"Stop!"

"You can't save everyone. It's an impossible thing. Think of us. Think of our future." She smiled up at him but there were tears in her eyes. "We have a wonderful future, so, please, please, my darling, come back inside, come back to our party."

He peeled her hands from his coat and pressed them together. "Party?" he repeated.

"Yes. *Our* party, darling."

He made a rough mocking sound as he set her firmly away from him. "Then do go back inside and enjoy the party, *darling*, but I have more important things to do."

He broke free and headed into the street, where men were hitching horses to wagons and organizing rescue teams. Marietta's fire department had already hitched their horses and was ready to go.

Sinclair was just about to climb up on the nearest wagon when yet another hand caught at his sleeve. "Sinclair," a soft voice said urgently.

He stiffened as McKenna stopped him. "Not you, too," he ground out.

Her chin lifted, her eyes almost black in the moonlight. "Take me with you. Let me go help."

"There is nothing you can do there. Stay here with the women."

"I might not be a nurse, but I know basic first aid. I

might be able to help. I want to help."

"You don't belong there. You'll just get in the way."

"Maybe, but it's my father's mine, and I'm still a Frasier. I am responsible for those men."

He cursed beneath his breath, but wasn't about to argue, because she was more right than she knew. Sinclair lifted her into the back of the wagon, placing her on top of a stack of blankets and sheets donated by Graff housekeeping, next to a rapidly growing pile of picks, axes, and shovels.

He flashed to other mine disasters from Butte. He remembered the tragedy from last summer. It was going to be a long night, and he wasn't thinking of himself, but the families of the men trapped below.

The fire wagons raced ahead of them. Marietta's doctor had been attending the party at the Graff, and he was in one of the wagons, while a member of the clergy was in another. Even in downtown Marietta, the glow of fire could be seen and anyone who could help was racing to the Frasier mining operations on Copper Mountain.

McKenna's teeth chattered during the ride up the mountain. She could smell the acrid smoke in the air and see the fiery glow ahead. She was cold, but more than that, afraid, worried for the wives who must be trying to stay calm since there was nothing else they could do.

In Butte, her father had sheltered his family from the accidents but, of course, she knew they happened. She'd avoided reading the newspaper accounts, not wanting to know the grisly details, not wanting to be more afraid for Sinclair than she already was.

The wagon wheels bumped across the railroad tracks. Empty railcars lined the track where it ended. The cars carried the ore to the smelters in Butte but no trains ran this late.

Sinclair was deep in discussion with the men in their wagon during the trip up. One of the men riding with them was the same person who'd burst into the ballroom to summon Sinclair. He was an Irishman in his mid-thirties, and he'd worked in the mines his entire life. He was supposed to work today but his wife had been in labor for over forty-eight hours and he'd stayed at her side, and because of that he'd escaped the blast.

"I would have been there otherwise," Patrick Sullivan said.

"Your wife?" Sinclair asked. "How is she?"

"The babe's arrived. It was a difficult delivery but she'll recover."

"She's not alone, is she?"

"No. Our oldest is with her. Mary's six. She's a good help."

Sinclair suddenly glanced at McKenna and she knew what he was saying. This is how it is here. This is how they live.

The roar of the fire grew louder as they got closer. In the distance she saw the mine's two headframes. One of the massive structures burned, while the wooden gallows and winding tower of the second was still untouched, and silhouetted by the moon. Her stomach cramped as she looked to the half dozen men gathered at the work site.

They were, she realized, waiting for Sinclair. He took charge immediately, too, directing the fire department to focus on the burning headframe while he organized a rescue party.

A big map of the Frasier mine had been spread flat on several planks of wood. Sinclair was gesturing to different places on the map, asking questions about the location of men at the various tunnels and for updates on the drifts themselves. When he'd managed the mine, the drifts weren't connected, which meant the men might survive if the rescue team acted quickly, because any smoke penetrating the tunnels could find an outlet, the draft drawing the smoke and gas out.

But if the drifts had been connected since he'd left, the smoke and gas would be pulled deeper into the mine and smother the men.

Patrick Sullivan said the drifts had not been connected.

Sinclair nodded. "Good. We need to get the fire out, and then we need to figure out exactly how many men are in each drift, and then I'm going in."

Men immediately began speaking and Sinclair silenced them. "I know everyone wants to help. These are your brothers, sons, and friends, but if you're married, and you have a family, you're not going with me. Only those without children will be allowed underground."

McKenna had only heard bits and pieces of the conversation but she did hear the last part. That only those without children would be going underground.

Sinclair planned to go underground.

He walked away with several men and she watched him, feeling helpless, and heartsick.

She shouldn't have come. She didn't want to be here for this. But, on the other hand, would she have been happier at the Graff, helping set up a makeshift hospital and waiting for updates?

At least here she knew what was happening. She wasn't getting reports through a secondary source.

Sinclair returned a few minutes later. He'd changed into work clothes, boots, and heavy trousers, but he was stripped to the waist, his powerful torso bare, muscles rippling beneath his skin. The men with him were all the same. Most carried heavy tools and a pack of some sort. Sinclair's pack was filled with explosives.

She watched him speak with one of the firemen, and then he talked to the Irishman who'd come for him at the Graff, and then he had words for another, and the entire time he talked, she looked at him, memorizing every detail, wanting to remember him like this. He was everything she'd thought he was, and more.

Strong. Brave. Good.

Emotion filled her. Her heart ached with all the things she wanted to say.

I love you.

I need you.

I can't live without you.

"McKenna."

He'd turned to find her, and she moved through the crowed.

"I need a promise from you," he said, calm despite the noise and mayhem around them.

If he was afraid, he didn't show it. She, on the other hand, was absolutely terrified.

"Yes?" she said, looking at his bare chest, remembering the place she'd touched on their ride home Thanksgiving night, remembering the hard, even beat of his heart beneath her hand.

"You must promise me that you will have the life you deserve. No matter what happens tonight, promise me. You will marry and have a family and have the life, the full life, the one you were always meant to have. Hear me?"

She blinked tears. "I hear you."

"No excuses. You're not a coward. You're to do it for me. And for you. For us, understand?"

"You're coming back."

"I hope. But if not, you've made me a promise. I expect you to keep it."

She blinked hard, clearing her eyes. "Only if you make

me one."

"And what's that, sweetheart?"

"*When* you come back, you're to marry me."

His blue eyes met hers and held. Thank God he said nothing about Ellie. He said nothing about broken engagements. He just looked at her and she felt the intensity of his gaze all the way through her.

"I need you," she added. "So come back. Come back to me. Please."

And then he was gone.

IT WAS A long night. Periodically the earth shook, and rocks would slide on the hillside as explosives were set off deep underground.

McKenna paced the length of the railroad track, too agitated to sit still. Twice the rescue operation succeeded in getting trapped miners out. Over a dozen miners had been freed but there were still a dozen plus men unaccounted for.

McKenna made herself useful as the doctor and his helpers bandaged cuts and cleaned wounds and set a broken leg. She listened as the men talked, explaining where they were, and how they were rescued. Sinclair and his men had reached them by tunneling from an abandoned mine shaft. The shaft had proved useless in terms of ore, but it was perfect for the emergency excavations.

A third group of men emerged from the abandoned shaft

and those outside cheered their appearance, and then moments later there was a giant explosion, and a miner was thrown across the site. Rocks went flying. The tunnel's entrance collapsed.

Someone called for help from inside the collapsed tunnel even as the ground began to shake again.

Miners dragged the rubble away from the tunnel entrance, and two members of the rescue team emerged, carrying a limp bloodied man. McKenna rushed forward. The man's head hung back, his black hair matted with blood.

Not Sinclair.

"How many more men down below still?" asked Patrick Sullivan.

"Four able to walk, two injured and in need of help, all at six hundred feet," answered one of the rescue team.

"And Douglas," added the other member of the rescue team. "But he ordered us out. It's not stable down there. He wants everyone off the mountain and into town. We're to leave a wagon for him, should he manage to get the others out."

"We can't just leave seven men six hundred feet down!"

"Not my call. Douglas is in charge. Move everyone out."

McKenna couldn't believe what she was hearing. She rushed to the map trying to make sense of the labyrinth of shafts and tunnels, wondering just how Sinclair was going to save the last men on his own.

A hand reached out and pointed to a spot. "He's here right now." The man tapped a dark mass on the map. "He's trying to get through there."

McKenna recognized the voice and looked up into the face of Mr. Finch. "Does he have a chance?"

"If anyone can do it, it's Douglas. He's the king of this mountain."

She searched his eyes. Mr. Finch wasn't slurring. He sounded sober. But she still had to ask, "Have you been drinking?"

"No, Miss Frasier."

"Is there anything I can do?"

"Keep praying."

THE MEN FORCED her off the mountain and into one of the departing wagons. She didn't want to go, and fought hard to remain, but none of the men listened.

She was driven to the Graff where many of the families had gathered to wait. The hotel's staff served coffee and tea and some of the hotel rooms had become hospital rooms for those wounded.

When needed, McKenna helped the doctor and nurse, and when she wasn't needed, she paced the corridors until she had to step outside and get fresh air.

The night seemed endless. Sometime close to dawn snowflakes began to slowly fall from the sky. There was no wind and they drifted gently, quietly, and McKenna stood in front of the hotel, holding her breath, praying.

Please, God, bring Sinclair home to me.

Please, God, you know my heart.

Please, God…

And then through the falling snow, she heard the clip-clop of hooves and the jingle of a harness as a big wagon came around the corner.

Men watching from the steps shouted. "It's the rest of them. Get the doctor! Get the stretchers. Let's get them in and get them warm."

IN THE DAYS to come, Sinclair would say he didn't do much, but everyone on the mountain that night knew if it weren't for Sinclair Douglas, all forty men would have died. He'd risked his life to save the shift.

McKenna didn't yet know any of this. She just knew the wagon with Sinclair had finally reached the Graff, and Mr. Graff himself came rushing out with the medical team to carry Sinclair and the other injured men into first floor rooms.

Ellie and her father weren't at the hotel any longer. There was no sign of the party that had taken place earlier. The only reminder of the earlier festivities was the beautiful fir tree in the lobby, its hundred candles now melted down.

McKenna paced outside Sinclair's room while the doctor

examined him, oblivious that her beautiful red gown was soiled and tattered, and then finally she was admitted to the room.

"This is quite improper," the doctor told her, looking at McKenna over her spectacles. "You're not his fiancée or a member of his family—"

"I know," McKenna interrupted wearily. "It's shocking behavior, but you can't be all that surprised. I'm America's most scandalous woman. So please step aside."

CHAPTER FOURTEEN

S HE STAYED WITH him at the Graff, never leaving his side, not even when Mrs. Douglas arrived midmorning and ordered her gone, stating she had no business being there when Sinclair was engaged to another woman.

McKenna quietly answered that she was staying, and the only person who could make her leave was Sinclair, and he was asleep.

"This isn't proper," Mrs. Douglas said.

"Yes, I'm aware of that."

"Have you thought about Miss Burnett's feelings?" Mrs. Douglas added.

"I have, but Miss Burnett is young and beautiful and will find another husband, whereas for me, there is only one man. There is only Sinclair."

"But he proposed to Miss Burnett, not you!"

"He also proposed to me first." Despite being dirty and disheveled, McKenna felt calmer then she had in months. "I love him, Mrs. Douglas. I love him with all of my heart and soul. I know you don't approve of me, but no woman will ever love your son as much as I do."

"You've certainly made a mess of things."

"I have, yes. Hopefully now I can make things better."

Ellie Burnett showed up at noon with her father. She looked elegant and pristine in a forest green dress with a delicate silk collar and cuffs. "You may go now," Ellie said, sweeping into the room, clearly not happy to see McKenna sitting on the bed. "Thank you for your nursing skills. Although I am not sure how hygienic you are."

McKenna didn't rise. She didn't bother with a smile, either. "I do not wish to be rude, Miss Burnett, but I will be blunt. Sinclair Douglas and I have had an understanding since I was eighteen. I am going to marry Mr. Douglas, not you. I can't end your engagement—only he can do that—but trust me, it is over."

"Do you realize everyone is talking about you, Miss Frasier? Do you realize they pity you?"

"I would be disappointed if they didn't talk. I am beyond scandalous."

"You will lose your job."

"Yes, I will."

"And you don't care?"

"I only care that it took this long for me to realize that there is nothing, and no one, I love more than Mr. Douglas."

Johanna arrived midafternoon. McKenna was exhausted and she squared her shoulders, prepared for another verbal skirmish.

But Johanna entered Sinclair's room quietly, and took a

seat in the available chair since McKenna was sitting on the bed next to her brother.

"They're saying dreadful things about you," Johanna said mildly. "You steal husbands and teach Thoreau and Walden and wear dirty dresses in the sick room."

McKenna frowned. "That's the worst they can say about me?"

"Well, there is the whole loss of virtue but that's old news."

"True."

Johanna's gaze was steady. "Why do you love him?"

For a second McKenna couldn't breathe, and then her shoulders lifted and fell. "He is the best person I know."

Johanna sighed. "You've made it very difficult to like you."

McKenna said nothing.

"But you've made it impossible to hate you. I can't stay angry with you. You love my brother. He loves you. You two should be together. But you can't fight for him in that disgusting dress. It's pathetic. You look tragic. If people are going to gossip about you, at least wear something newsworthy." Johanna's lips curved wryly. "I have provided a newsworthy dress. It's in a room down the hall. I also encourage you to bathe while you're changing. I'll stay with Sinclair until you return."

A lump filled McKenna's throat. She was exhausted and overwhelmed. "You've been so angry with me."

"I have. I hated that you hurt Sinclair. You disappointed him… and you disappointed me, because we *were* friends, and then you just forgot about us. All of us." She paused, glancing from McKenna to Sinclair where he lay bandaged and still. "But maybe it's time to let bygones be bygones and start fresh as I understand there's a strong possibility that you'll soon be joining the family."

"I guess I need to make sure it's what Sinclair wants."

Johanna's eyes widened. "Oh, it's what Sinclair wants. Trust me."

TIRED, SO TIRED he couldn't open his eyes. Tired, and sore. It hurt to move. It hurt to breathe.

What had happened to him?

And then Sinclair remembered. The explosion at the mine. The trapped men. The party. McKenna.

He stiffened, his hand jerking out to the side. He touched something warm.

Eyes opening he struggled to focus. Cloud dark hair. Pale beautiful face. Sleeping.

McKenna. Here. McKenna here with him.

Had he died and gone to heaven?

He drew a breath, wincing at the burn in his chest, and the searing white-hot pain in his ribs. He didn't think he'd feel this bad in heaven. That meant he was still on earth, but Mac was with him. Still.

Maybe there was heaven on earth...

He thought back to the promises they'd made at the mine. Had she really meant what she'd said? That if he came back, she'd marry him?

Was his girl going to finally to be his wife?

If that was all it took—almost dying—why hadn't he almost killed himself years ago?

Smiling faintly, Sinclair closed his eyes, and gave himself back up to sleep.

IT WAS LATE in the evening when Sinclair opened his eyes and McKenna was there, sleeping next to him on the bed, waiting for the moment he'd awake. She felt him stir and she pushed herself up on her elbow.

"How are you feeling?" she whispered, gently pushing dark blond hair back from his bruised forehead.

"Where are we?" He rasped.

"The hotel. They brought all the injured men here after the explosion."

"How long have you been here?"

"A day and night."

"You've stayed here with me this entire time?"

She nodded. "Yes."

He stirred, his arm slowly extending to curve around her. "Ah, sweetheart, that will make people talk."

"And they are, but I had to stay. It's my job to protect

you." She leaned over and kissed him carefully, trying not to touch any place that had a cut or welt. But even with the bruises he was beautiful.

"Protecting me from what?"

"Women who don't deserve you."

The corner of his mouth curved. His eyes smiled at her, too. "Sounds like you've been handling things while I've been sleeping."

"Oh, I have. I let everyone know just how things are."

"And just how are things?"

"It's you and me. Forever."

"That means marriage, sweet girl."

"I know. I'm forcing you to marry me. I'm sorry."

He reached up and drew her head down to his, kissing her lightly. His eyes closed and he drew a deep breath. "Stay with me, Mac."

"Always."

He exhaled. "I hurt."

"Not surprised. You have broken bones. Your shoulder, your wrist, maybe some ribs, but I'm told it won't slow you down too much." She leaned over him and kissed him again, murmuring, "Apparently you are the king of Copper Mountain."

"That's because you're the queen."

AFTER HELPING THE doctor change Sinclair's bandages, she

made sure Sin ate some dinner and then he just wanted to sleep some more. McKenna still wouldn't go home. She curled up next to Sinclair and slept next to him all night, only leaving when it was morning and Sinclair was stirring and she wanted to make sure he had some food in him before his next dose of medicine.

She was just returning, having ordered a tray of milk, eggs, and toast for Sinclair when she heard voices coming from Sinclair's room. McKenna cautiously pushed the door open and then froze.

Her father was there, standing next to the bed.

She looked from her father, to Sinclair, and then back to her father.

Beyond shocked, McKenna went weak all over. She leaned against the doorframe. It wasn't proper. A lady didn't lean. A lady was always calm and composed.

She wasn't a lady.

"Hello, Father," she said, her voice husky.

"I heard you were creating a scene," he said.

"Plural, Father. Scenes. It's what I do."

"So I've learned." He sounded resigned rather than outraged. "Can we have a word in the hall?"

McKenna glanced to the bed. She gave Sinclair a tight smile before stepping from the room. Her father followed, closing the door behind them.

For a moment there was just silence and then he spoke. "You look well," he said. "Considering."

She'd been studying him as well. He was leaner, while his beard was fuller, and whiter. "You, too."

"It's been what? Nine months? Ten?"

"About that." She paused. "I'm surprised to see you."

"The accident is in all the papers."

"There will be a lawsuit, won't there?"

"Nearly all accidents are the result of human error. The company is rarely held accountable and, in this case, there is no negligence on management. You should be fine."

"I'm not worried. I've been disinherited."

He gave her a curious look. "You don't know, do you?"

"Know what, Father?"

"It's not my mine. It's yours." His dark eyes bored into her. "I put it in your name last summer. It belongs to you. It's been yours all this time."

"But there's no income—"

"There's plenty of income. It's deposited right into the bank there on Main Street. You have an account in your name. Mr. Bramble manages the funds on your behalf."

"I didn't know that."

"I told Douglas if he married you, I'd put the deed of the mine in your name, which, by marriage, would make it his."

"But he didn't marry me."

He shrugged. "I don't know why."

"Maybe he didn't want to be forced into a marriage." McKenna held his gaze. "That was a terrible thing you did, dangling me like that. I don't appreciate it."

"He didn't, either. I felt badly later. That's why I went ahead and put the deed in your name after all."

"And you weren't going to tell me?"

"I wanted to see if you could make it on your own, and you did."

She couldn't believe it, but he actually sounded proud. "I don't want your money, Father. I want your love."

"Funny, that is exactly what Sinclair said about you." He pulled out his pocket watch and checked the time. "Incidentally, it's bad form to threaten a young lady."

"I didn't threaten anyone."

"The Texan's daughter."

"I was quite civil but firm and let her know that she wasn't going to marry Mr. Douglas, as he and I had a previous understanding." Her chin lifted. "And we did. I promised years ago to marry him."

"I know. He asked me for your hand years ago."

"And you said no."

"I did. But after your disgrace, I approached him and made him an offer. I'd make him a partner if he married you. He refused."

McKenna had heard all this before but it still hurt. "He told me."

"What makes you think he'll marry you now?"

"I've grown up." She hesitated. "I know what's important. I don't need the whole world. I just need Sinclair."

Her father turned away, hands on his hips. "Your mother

warned me that I indulged you too much and then I sent you to that school—"

"School didn't ruin me. And you didn't ruin me." She reached out and touched his arm carefully. "I've been my own person my entire life. And I made a mistake in New York, thinking I could be free, and I'm sorry I embarrassed you, and embarrassed Mary, but my life is a good life, and Father, I'm happy. I love Sinclair, and I am right where I should be. Please forgive me. Please?"

He was silent so long she didn't think he was going to answer, and then he said flatly, "I've only loved three people in my life. Your mother is gone, and when I cut you off, it felt like another death. I do forgive you, but McKenna, it will never be the way it was. Not for me. Not for anyone."

She drew a slow breath. "Does that mean you'll give me away at my wedding?"

"If I can, I will. When is the wedding?"

"Soon. Sinclair wants a Christmas wedding."

"That's just a few days from now."

She nodded. "I know. I'm worried it's too soon for him, considering the pain he's in, but it's what he wants, and I'm not about to tell him no."

"I can't be here for Christmas. I'm taking Mary to New York. If you want to wait—"

"I can't do that to Sinclair, Father."

"I'm sorry then. But I've promised Mary she'll have Christmas on Fifth Avenue this year. She's been invited to a number of New Year's parties."

McKenna tried to smash the disappointment. "You don't think she'd love Christmas in Marietta?"

"She's ready to enter society."

"I understand." She gave him a quick hug and then stepped back. "Thank you for coming, Father. It was good to see you. I've missed you."

He blinked, his eyes suddenly suspiciously bright. "Goodbye, my daughter."

CHAPTER FIFTEEN

T HEY MARRIED AT St. James on Christmas Eve between the five o'clock and midnight services. Sinclair still ached, the cold making the broken bones throb, but he'd had enough gossip and was ready to make McKenna his wife.

He hated that McKenna's family could not attend, but his mother and Johanna were there, and they were both well on their way to accepting McKenna as part of the family. Johanna had made McKenna a stunning bridal gown, and McKenna reciprocated by asking Johanna to be her maid of honor.

The Brambles attended the service, as did the Zabrinskis, the Parkers, and the Hoffmans.

McKenna had asked Albert Graff if he'd be willing to give her away since her father couldn't be there, and Mr. Graff was so touched he insisted on hosting the wedding dinner for them afterwards even though Christmas Eve was already a very busy time for him at the hotel.

When McKenna and Sinclair arrived at the Graff after the church ceremony, Sinclair expected a small dinner for twenty in the restaurant, but instead the ballroom was filled with the miners and their families, all wearing their Sunday best.

The miners cheered as they entered the ballroom, every man rising to his feet. The applause was deafening. Sinclair stood in the doorway, rooted to the spot.

McKenna squeezed his arm and smiled up at him. "I had to invite them. You saved them, but they saved us."

"Albert can't be expected to pay for all of this."

"He's not. I am."

"You are?"

She nodded. "Mr. Bramble told me what I had in my account, and I thought that we needed to have the community here with us. It's our celebration, and they are our people."

Sinclair shook his head, overwhelmed. He thought he knew her and yet she constantly surprised him. "This is the best present you could give me."

"I love you, Sin."

"And I love you, Mac."

"Even though I have a rebellious heart and progressive soul?"

His chest tightened, aching with emotion. She had no idea how much he loved her. He'd waited fifteen years for this night. "It's the part of you I love most."

WITH SINCLAIR NOT yet able to travel, they decided to wait

until summer to take a honeymoon, but Sinclair wasn't about to let his injuries keep him from moving McKenna into his house.

McKenna loved his house.

She loved how the house was situated on the land with sweeping views of the valley and the snowcapped mountains. The house was warm, with a stove in every room and Sinclair had plans to bring electricity into the valley for the ranching families.

McKenna didn't mind the lack of electricity, though. After her rustic cabin, Sinclair's two-story house felt like a mansion. The downstairs had big rooms but her favorite place was upstairs. She loved sleeping in his bed and making love at night in the second story room in the wash of white moonlight.

She was happy, so very happy. Not just because she was finally with Sinclair, but because she could see how happy he was, too. Not just with her, but with his life. He was a man that loved the land, and he relished his work, spending long hours outside, putting up fences, seeing to his livestock, making sure his ranch prospered. He had a significant piece of land, too, and he'd earned it himself. He was a self-made man—like her father—but at the same time, he was so very different from her father.

She loved Sinclair's courage and admired his convictions, and in her letters to her friends she wrote of her love for her new husband and how blessed she felt, and how grateful.

LATE JANUARY, MCKENNA received a small pile of letters in the mail. There was one from Amelia, and one from her sister Mary, and then a third from a publisher in Philadelphia.

McKenna read the letters from Amelia and Mary, so very glad to hear from both. Mary had written to extend her congratulations to McKenna on her marriage and even though Mary's letter was brief, it was a start, and McKenna felt hope as well as relief.

McKenna waited to open the third envelope, though, wanting Sinclair there when she did.

It was hard to be patient but finally he was back in from his evening chores and after she made him evening tea, she carried the envelope to the table.

"Do you know what this is?" she asked him.

He reached up to push a long strand of hair behind her ear. "No."

"It's from The Curtis Publishing Company in Philadelphia," she said, trying to contain her excitement. "I *think* they're writing to tell me they want to publish my letters."

"So why haven't you opened it?"

"Because it could also be rejection."

"Will you be so terribly disappointed if it is?"

"No," she said, not sounding very convincing at all.

He smiled and reached for her, drawing her down on his lap. "It sounds to me as if you will be disappointed if it doesn't work out."

She shrugged, snuggling closer. "I miss teaching. The writing keeps me from getting bored."

"There are other publishers."

"Or I could open my own school."

"Or you could open your own school—" He broke off and frowned. "Wait. Do you really want to do something like that? Become a Superintendent Egan?"

"No. But I don't necessarily think men should be the only ones in charge of education."

"Oh dear, it sounds as if you're about to march for more reforms," he said smiling at her and, as always, his gorgeous blue eyes smiled, too. "Open your letter, sweetheart, put me out of misery. Let's see what your publisher has to say."

McKenna held her breath as she opened the envelope and withdrew a folded sheet of paper. Something fluttered out as she unfolded the stationery. McKenna reached for the paper even as she scanned the letter. "They want my letters." Her voice broke and she looked up at Sinclair, pulse racing. "They're going to turn them into a regular column."

"Who is the offer from?"

"Edward Bok. He's the new editor of *Ladies Home Journal*, and he and Mrs. Louisa Knapp, the magazine's founder, think… oh, let me read just read it to you, 'We are delighted to offer you a contract as we believe your column would be an excellent addition to the magazine.'" McKenna laughed and hugged the letter to her chest. "I'm going to be published!"

He kissed her. "Well done, Mac."

"And they're paying me," she added, finding the check that had fluttered out "Two dollars per column. They've sent me a check for the first four already."

"And I thought you'd finally reconciled yourself to being dependent on me," he teased.

"Living out here, I am dependent on you for everything but, you must admit, it's nice for me to have my own pocket money."

LATE THAT NIGHT after they'd made love and lay side by side, cocooned under the layers of blankets topped by the quilt McKenna had made, she stirred in Sinclair's arms, unable to stop thinking about something that had been bothering her for a long time.

"Sin, are you asleep?" she whispered.

"No, not yet," he answered, his deep husky.

"Never mind. We'll talk tomorrow."

"What's troubling you?"

"Nothing—"

He sat up, punching the pillow behind his back. "Let's talk now. Tell me."

She turned to face him, her hand going to his chest, her palm over his heart to feel the steady beating. "I hate the mine." She drew a quick breath. "I hate it so much. Do we need the income? If so—"

"We don't need the income."

"I've never asked you about your finances but I trust you and don't want to be a burden."

"You're not a burden, and I appreciate that you didn't marry me for my money, but my investments are doing quite well, and the mine is yours. I don't want any part of it."

She was silent a long time. She kept her hand pressed to his heart, feeling the steady even beat all the way through her.

He was her rock. Her roots. He hugged the ground so she could stretch and fly.

"I want to sell it." McKenna felt a little queasy saying the words aloud, but it's what she'd been thinking ever since she heard the news that her father had put the Marietta mine in her name. "I don't like it. But it's something you've done nearly all your life and I don't want to sell it if you'll miss that connection."

"I won't miss it. It's not a connection I need. Not at all."

"What about the money when I sell?"

"It's *your* money."

"Do you want to know what I'm going to do with the money?"

"No. Let's find a buyer and then surprise me."

She shifted in his arms and put her cheek to his chest. His body was so warm. She loved his strength, and the confidence he had in her.

His love made all things possible.

His love gave her courage, and hope that one day the world would be a better place for all.

"Thank you for making me the sun," she said, blinking back tears.

"The sun and the stars and all the universe."

She blinked again and a tear slipped and fell, trickling onto his bare chest. "You lifted me up instead of smashing me down."

"Ah, sweetheart, I will never let anyone smash you. We need our dreamers and thinkers."

"And I need you." She lifted her head and reached up to kiss him. "I need you, Sinclair Douglas, forever."

"Done."

Epilogue

MCKENNA SOLD THE copper mine in the spring of 1890 to a Mr. William Schafer from Reno, Nevada, and then used a significant portion of the proceeds to build the first hospital in Marietta, and the rest to create a fund to help take care of the families that worked in the mine, for as long as the mine was in existence.

McKenna spent the early parts of the summer working with the architect commissioned to draw the plans for the new hospital. The new hospital would be built across the river from the courthouse, with access to the train depot and would be one of the most modern hospitals built in Montana outside Butte.

She continued writing her columns for the *Ladies Home Journal,* and practiced her cooking, which sadly, was still not a strength.

Fortunately, Sinclair hadn't married her for her domestic arts and seemed perfectly content with his progressive wife who loved her books, and was currently reading everything McKenna could find on infants and parenting, determined to be prepared for October when the new little Douglas,

239

their Hallowe'en baby, arrived.

Away in Montana, life was very, very good.

No, make that exceptional.

THE END

You won't want to miss the next book in the
Paradise Valley Ranch series

Married in Montana

Coming soon – June 2017

Beautiful, spirited, Texas born Ellie Burnett needs a husband. Fast. Her father, rancher Archibald Burnett, is dying, and she's determined to marry to protect the ranch and preserve her father's legacy in Montana's rugged Paradise Valley. The trouble is, she wants to wear the boots in the family and the man she has in mind, Irishman Thomas Sheenan would never stand for that.

Independent and taciturn Thomas Sheenan isn't looking for a wife, having spent far too much of his life taking care of others. He's come to Montana to carve out his own identity, and be his own man. The last thing he needs is a headstrong bride, but when Ellie approaches him with the offer of a lifetime, he can't refuse.

Thomas didn't anticipate falling for his new bride. He moved to Montana to stake his claim…he never planned on losing his heart.

Find out more information here
janeporter.com

The Paradise Valley Ranch Series

Book 1: *Away in Montana*

Book 2: *Married in Montana*
Coming soon – June 2017

Book 3: *Home in Montana*
Coming soon – Winter 2018

Check out *New York Times* bestselling author Jane Porter's
contemporary romance series....

The Taming of the Sheenans

The Sheenans are six powerful wealthy brothers from
Marietta, Montana. They are big, tough, rugged men, and as
different as the Montana landscape.

Christmas at Copper Mountain
Book 1: Brock Sheenan's story

Tycoon's Kiss
Book 2: Troy Sheenan's story

The Kidnapped Christmas Bride
Book 3: Trey Sheenan's story

Taming of the Bachelor
Book 4: Dillion Sheenan's story

A Christmas Miracle for Daisy
Book 5: Cormac Sheenan's story

The Lost Sheenan's Bride
Book 6: Shane Sheenan's story

Available now at your favorite online retailer!

About the Author

New York Times and USA Today bestselling author of forty-nine romances and women's fiction titles, **Jane Porter** has been a finalist for the prestigious RITA award five times and won in 2014 for Best Novella with her story, Take Me, Cowboy, from Tule Publishing. Today, Jane has over 12 million copies in print, including her wildly successful, Flirting With Forty, picked by Redbook as its Red Hot Summer Read, and reprinted six times in seven weeks before being made into a Lifetime movie starring Heather Locklear. A mother of three sons, Jane holds an MA in Writing from the University of San Francisco and makes her home in sunny San Clemente, CA with her surfer husband and two dogs.

Thank you for reading

Away in Montana

If you enjoyed this book, you can find more from all our great authors at TulePublishing.com, or from your favorite online retailer.

TULE
PUBLISHING

Made in the USA
Middletown, DE
28 February 2019